Intertwined

to Care | to Love | to Heal

Verkeya Lanece

Prepared by: Ebony Nicole Smith Consulting, LLC |
www.ebonynicolesmith.com

Edited by: Massawa Stevens – Morrison

Book Cover Designed by: Massawa Stevens – Morrison

Author's Photo: Kelon Miller, Creative Elements Photography

ISBN: 978-0-578-69744-4

Dedication

This book is dedicated to those people who remain hopeful, even when all seems lost.

Do not be anxious about anything, but in every situation, by prayer and petition, with thanksgiving, present your requests to God. And the peace of God, which transcends all understanding, will guard your hearts and your minds in Christ Jesus.

Philippians 4:6-7

Contents

Acknowledgments

My village is deep and the Smoove way that everyone has jumped in, prayed and supported my first book endeavor fills my heart.

Veronica and Kevin, Valen and Keynon, Dana (thanks for sharing some of your story) and Teisha and my awesome nieces, Khia and Maddy and nephew, Nichopieces. I am so glad that God made us family.

Coach Ebony Nicole of Ebony Nicole Smith Consulting, for all of your calls, emails and text and for the hard work you put in to get me through this process.

Many thanks to Minister Sue, for wearing several hats throughout this process. Always ready to jump in and never failing to give an encouraging word.

Thank you Kelon, Creative Elements Photography for making me look my best and creating a positive and fun atmosphere to be photographed.

Sisters Uptown Bookstore, LLC, Kori and Mama Jan for encouraging me to put pen to paper and providing a space where I could share my poetry.

Michael Millington, Articulate Literature and Media, LLC.

Thanks Joshua, Na'imah, Ms. Yvette, Quaneisha and Genine, your voices were invaluable.

My Bonus brothers and sisters…Michael, David, Jason, LaShona, Kwana, Denesha, Carlyne, Iris, Stacey, Josephine and Tiffany.

Friendships are invaluable…Kim B., Kim A. Latasha, Sheana, and Dawn.

The Strong, Holman, Horn, Woods, Lewis and McLean Clans… You have all influenced me in more ways than can be imagined.

The Creggs… Love you. Sleep in Peace, Stacey.

The best teacher ever, Ms. Loyd-Blackman. Thank you even now for being part of my village.

Charles, in a time where it is apparent that the color of our skin is not valued in the country our foreparents built and we live in, I see you! You are valued! Thanks for ensuring that I stayed healthy enough to complete this.

Most of all, to my baby angel, Kaleb and my active baby Kaiden. Mommy Loves you both the most, but God loves you best.

To all those who took a chance on purchasing my book, thank you. I hope that it has provoked your thinking and fostered some conversations.

Intertwined

Part 1

Kasey & Justin

Despite the Challenges

Kasey

Always having *verbal intercourse* with this man until the early morning hours knowing full well that I needed to get up at 7am for work. It didn't make the calls end sooner. I kept saying I wouldn't let him keep me on the phone into the late night (technically early morning) but it happened anyway. It all happened so fast, the hold he has on my heart.

We met on a warm Saturday in April while I was running on one of my favorite routes, the West Side Highway. As I got ready to turn around to head home, this garbage truck pulled up in front of me. I waited for it to pass me by so I could complete my routine. It jerked a few times, as if he was trying to get my attention. I jogged in place to prepare to continue my course when I was frozen in my tracks at the sight of this caramel skinned, chiseled armed brother that said good afternoon after jumping down off the truck. I had my music on and up pretty loud but read his full lips and responded kindly with, "Hi." I removed my headphones to hear what else he had to say.

"My name is Justin and yours?"

His partner went on about his business, but obviously ear hustled because he kept looking over his shoulders with a smirk. I was taken aback by his forward yet polite introduction and felt unsure of my body because I'd already got half my run in.

"I'm Kasey." I didn't offer my hand.

"Nice to meet you. Do you always run this route?"

"Most days."

"So, how do I contact you to give you company on your next run?"

"I run alone." I was steadily attempting to end this conversation, but he was persistent.

"Then how do I get to know you?" I said to him, "Get creative!" and I made a run for it.

After that day, I never really gave Justin a second thought. I was focused on establishing myself as a Family Court Legal Services (FCLS) attorney in Manhattan Family Court and believe me it was, no easy task. After six months on the job some of the judges were still not so nice and some were downright mean. My supervising attorney, thankfully, was a pretty awesome woman who was willing to be my mentor, which is a rare thing in this business. As spring continued so too did my running. I was training for a triathlon and the running was the most grueling part because I'd found that passion later in life. I was a swimmer since high school. I felt safe in the water, swimming was second nature to me. Two weeks after our first brief encounter, I heard a honk from a garbage truck which startled me.

"Finally!"

I turned to see a smiling face with nice teeth glistening in the sun to match his sexy voice. He leaned forward on the steering wheel, "I see you again. I have been begging to be kept on this same route just to see you again." I have to admit I was flattered that he had taken such measures to ensure he would see me again.

"Well, you see me. Now what?" I adjusted my tank top that was slightly falling off my shoulder and pulled up my leggings. This time I wasn't so worried about my appearance because, truthfully, I was in the best shape I had been in since high school. He reached into his side pocket and pulled out a little white card.

"Look, here is my number Kasey. I'd like to get to know you." To me he was confident and sure of himself. I found that to be attractive. Taking the business card from him, I glance at his fingers. Despite his career as a sanitation worker, his fingernails weren't dirty or in need of a manicure. On top of that, he remembered my name. These impressive details were grabbing my attention. The card read:

Justin Thompson
646.409.8132
JThompson@gmail.com

I flipped the card.

JT Tax Preparation

In the same fashion as when we first met, “Thanks. I have to go now.” I ran for it and then I heard, “Hey! Wait! Kasey!”

I yelled back, “What? I have to finish my run.”
“Are you going to call me?”
“It’s still early in the day. You’ll just have to wait and see.”

Justin

After waiting two long weeks to see this woman, I finally gave her my business card. I hoped she would call. I wasn’t in the business of picking up women, but it was something about this one that I just had to get to know her. I mean, she was beautiful, about five feet four inches, her skin tone eluded to her mixed heritage, shapely, short cut and seemingly educated. I had been single for quite some time and was ready to begin dating again. Married previously; it wasn’t my finest hour. We were young and I wasn't ready to be a husband. I was still running with my boys instead of making my marriage my priority. We remained friends and there were no hard feelings. Shayla, my ex, had since remarried and had two beautiful children. I was starting to feel that I wanted some of that. This beautiful girl named Kasey was giving me thoughts of family and what that could be like. Instead of calling, she sent a text at about 8pm on a Tuesday night. It read:

If you're not busy, call me. Not sure of your hours and didn't want to disturb your sleep.

Seeing the message, I immediately called because my days off were Wednesday & Thursday and hell, even if they weren't, I would have still called. After about two rings she answered and I didn't know what was going on with me but I was sweating, my heart was beating fast and my mouth suddenly felt like cotton. I couldn't believe this woman was making me nervous.

"Kasey."

"Justin. I guess you weren't busy?" I found her voice soothing.

"No, how are you?"

"Just got settled in from work. I thought before I got ready to unwind, I'd try to contact you." She sounded like she had a long day, but I was happy to hear from her. I tried to mask my excitement and nervousness. It was like the first time I had spoken to a girl on the phone. I didn't want to sound like I was nervous and eager. I tried to temper that by allowing her to lead the conversation. After about five minutes, I felt calmer.

It was easy to talk to Kasey. The conversation felt like I was chatting with an old friend that I had reconnected with. She made me laugh, which was refreshing for once. She wasn't completely open; I could tell because some topics she skimmed over. I could tell she was feeling me out just as I was doing to her. She told me about her life; not enough for me to say I knew her, but just enough to make me want to see her sooner than later and spend time getting to know her.

All time was lost while conversing because we had been on the phone for about two hours before either of us realized.

"So, see you Sunday?" I had asked her to have brunch with me. I wasn't going to wait it out like I would normally do. I felt I had to move fast but, be strategic in my movements. I only hope she likes my pace.

"Yes, Sunday. I hope to hear from you before then."

"Of course, you will. I wouldn't miss a conversation with you for the world."
We ended our call but I could have kept talking or listening to her. I couldn't wait for Sunday to arrive. But as long as I had the open to stay in contact with her, I was good.

Kasey

He picked me up in his silver Dodge Charger. I'm impressed because I had no idea what to expect. I wore a multicolored dress of orange and yellow and some strappy wedge sandals. I attempted to keep things classy, but not over the top. The goal was to make sure my attire would be suitable for wherever he decided to take me. I had already come from church and he didn't say where we were going. When I got in the car, I was even more surprised. This man was just the antithesis of what I expected. Not only did he get out of the car and open the door for me, but the music that was playing took me back to a beautiful memory of my high school music class, The Exploration of Jazz. I was expecting to hear Jay-Z or something of that nature playing, however Miles Davis' *Kind of Blue* was coming through the speakers.

"You okay? You have a very puzzled look on your face." He turned down the volume a bit from his steering wheel.

"I am surprised that's all. I love Miles Davis." I bopped my head slightly to the horns and piano as Freedie Freeloader played.

"I love all kinds of music."
"I see. I like various kinds of music, but there are some genres I stay clear of."
"Nothing wrong with variety, is there?"
"No. No there isn't. Just don't particularly love heavy metal or country."
"I hear you. Not particularly fond of those genres either." He laughed.
"Where are we off to?"
"I made reservations at Calle Ocho. Have you ever been there?"
"No, but think I've heard of it. It's on 81st street, correct?"
"Yes, in the hotel. It used to be on Amsterdam Avenue but they moved it." The car conversation was mainly about music. He seemed to like a lot of music from the 70's era, The Sylistics, Al Green, Otis Redding and The Chi-Lites to name a few. I liked that he wasn't just into contemporary rap music. He was amused when I said that I was into some pop artists like Justin Timberlake and Pink. I told him I love to dance to house music which caused him to laugh as he couldn't envision me dancing to it.

"I dance really well to salsa but, my aunts and uncle would call me a disgrace if I couldn't."
"It's that deep?"
"Justin, you have no idea. Not knowing salsa in my family is like a black person not knowing the Electric Slide at a wedding."
"Touché."
We laughed. His laughter was welcoming and made me feel like I could be myself.

I was checking Justin out on the way to the restaurant. He was adorned in blue denim jeans, a burnt orange button up and a pair of tan Oxford Brutini shoes. This man was making me think all kinds of things, like what was under those clothes. My expectations had already been exceeded with his charming personality.

We found street parking and walked the short distance to the restaurant. Justin's scent was intoxicating and I recognized the Aqua di Gio. I would know that cologne anywhere, my brother wore it. Kind of strange, yet it was familiar, comforting. We got inside and were immediately escorted to our table. I loved the ambiance and colors of Calle Ocho. It made me feel alive, like I was in a Frida Khalo painting. Hot pink, blue, orange and green adorned the walls and pillars throughout the restaurant. The salsa and merengue blasting through the speakers and the sounds of all the patrons enjoying sangria, food and conversation.

Justin

Kasey was a beautiful woman, but on this day I got to take her all in. She wore makeup, but it was subtle. She was in this dress that not only showed her curves but made me want to undress her and enjoy her body from head to toe. We sat down in the booth and she asked how I knew about this place. I told her I'd been coming here for some time because I love the food.

"This is your *first date* place?" She asked the question while looking down at the menu. She must have been thinking that since it was my favorite place, this is where I take every woman on a first date.

"No, I haven't dated in a long time." I felt the need to be honest with her because I felt this connection, although she was making me work for it. "I was once married---"

Kasey quickly interrupted, "Isn't this heavy first date conversation?"

"I feel secure enough to be honest. Like I said, I was married. She and I are friends, but I learned some hard lessons getting married at 23 years old."

"That is young." She closed the menu to give me her full attention, which I appreciated.

"Yes, I wasn't ready for all that a husband should do and be." We ordered our sangrias and food then continued to talk.

"Would you marry again?"

"I would like to and hope to find someone to share my life with. One day she will walk into my life…or run." She raised her eyebrow and smiled. I think she got that I was hinting that she could be that person.

"Can I ask you a question, now?"

"Sure, you can ask me anything you want. What you ask will determine if I answer it or not." Witty and sassy…Damn this woman!

"Why are you single?" I hope she got the indication that I'm not dating just to be dating but, to find the woman I want to share my life with.

"I came back to New York after law school and my ex and I decided that we were going in different paths. It was a mutual agreement to move on."

Our drinks arrived and we toasted to a great evening and, "To the start of something beautiful," I added. Still inquisitive about her life, I asked, "What kind of law do you practice?"

"I'm an attorney for family court."

"Must be interesting and difficult at times."

"Honestly, I feel like I'm in over my head,", Kasey responded. "Between the stuff I'm being exposed to and dealing with the nuances of being on the job, I've questioned my abilities on occasion." For the first time since we met, I saw a little bit of her vulnerability. I didn't want to push her so I moved the conversation along.

"I know you aren't an only child. Tell me more about your family."

Before Kasey could answer, our food arrived to the table. We paused to allow the waiter to move away before we continued our conversation. We also ordered different sangria. I felt like she was enjoying herself and it was obvious that the sangria was allowing her inhibitions to dissipate just a bit.

"So, tell me about your family." I asked again in case it was forgotten due to the interruption.

"I have a huge family. My mom has four brothers and one sister. They migrated from Puerto Rico as children. My dad is one of four. His parents are from Charleston, South Carolina. My parents kept it small, so it's just my brother Kyle and I. We're very close and grew up thick as thieves. I hate that he lives so far away sometimes. He's married with two sons. Where he was, I was sure to follow. What about you?" She looked sad, like a memory of the two of them came to the forefront of her thoughts.

"It is obvious that you miss him." At that moment I knew her brother's opinion and approval would be key. "I'm an only child and it mostly has been just my dad and I. My mom passed from lymphoma when I was 10."

"I'm sorry to hear that. I can't imagine what that must have been like."

"It was a long time ago." Again, I could see vulnerability and compassion. Her eyes were so telling. They were green with flecks of hazel. It was easy to tell her things because you could feel the trust from her eyes.

As the afternoon flowed on, I ordered a dessert called *The Bombas*. From the way Kasey bit into each piece of the sweet dough, lightly powdered with sugar and sauces for dipping, I could see that Calle Ocho would become our favorite spot. The rest of brunch was lighthearted chatter and I didn't want to end our time together. I also didn't want to assume she felt the same. I felt this need to be close to her. Heart racing again, mouth feeling of cotton, I asked, "Do you need to get home or can we spend more time talking."

"I'd love to keep talking." That was just what I wanted to hear.

****

Central Park was just a block away so we went there enjoying the views of bikers, runners and each other. After walking a few ways into the park, we found a bench underneath a leafy green tree. There was still much more I wanted to know about his woman.

"What kind of movies are you interested in? Please don't say *RomComs.*"

"How did you know?" Kasey remarked. "Just kidding, I like action movies mostly. Very much into comics. Grew up on them because of Kyle."

I enjoyed the evening until it came to a close. While I didn't want it to end, it gave me something to look forward to.

Kasey

I was still smelling the scent of his cologne and feeling a little intoxicated from that Spanish Harlem sangria. I had let my guard down with Justin and that put me on edge. He felt safe and I didn't quite like that I was feeling this so soon. After such a long relationship with Sam, I wasn't ready to walk down that road again. But I kind of liked it, even though it frightened me slightly. I would have to wait on the outcome, but I was not rushing into anything.

A new day was here and I needed to ready myself for the hellish day in front of me. As I attempted to prepare, I could not stop thinking about Justin. I was ready to kiss his lips but I didn't want to give him the impression that it was okay to take liberties with my body yet. As I was taking out clothes, my phone rang from across the room. Knowing the ringtone, I wasn't in a hurry to answer it, but did since *she* was calling.

"Hey mom!" I answered sprightly.

"You sound like you're in a good mood. What are you up to?"

"Getting ready for tomorrow."

"I hope you have a date for the wedding next month. I wish you would settle down and give me some grandchildren."

"Mom, you have grandchildren."

"Yes, two boys. I'd like a girl." My mother and I had this conversation at least once a month since I finished law school. It didn't help that my god sister, Clarke, was getting married in a month and that my cousins kept getting married and poppin' out babies. I wished she would've left me be and allowed life to happen. Did I think about marriage and children? Yes! I just felt I like obsessing over it wasn't healthy. Besides, being 28, I had some time and my career was important to me. I wasn't in the mood to address her concerns about my life. I was happy with the way it was going and if it was meant to be it would be. At the time, I wanted to keep my focus on my work.

"Mom, I will talk to you soon. I love you." I had to get off the phone with her before I got really upset. I showered; put on my night clothes, turned off the light and my phone buzzes... It was from Justin.

It was a beautiful day and I'm glad I spent it with you. Sleep Well.

Justin

Kasey didn't respond to my text and I figured it was because she was sleeping. I just wanted her to know she was in my thoughts. When I got up to get ready for work, I realized that thoughts of her had never left. I kept envisioning her in that dress nicely fitting her body and showing all the right spots. I kept imagining kissing her and tasting her tongue. I had to quiet the thoughts because *Lil Man* was becoming hard.

It must have been just past 9:30am and my phone buzzed.

Had a great time. See you soon.

Eager to see her, I wasted no time and asked her for another date. I didn't want to give anyone else a chance to swoop in and grab her attention.

It had been quite a while since a woman had made me smile with anticipation. We spoke every day since our first date. The late-night conversation was always good. The next week we hung out again and there was this magnetism between us. We were walking through Palisades Mall and as we walked, we got close and our hands brushed up against one another. Without hesitation, Kasey took my hand into hers. This date we did something neither of us knew how to do: bowl. Our scores were 89 and 95. There were lots of gutter balls, but it was fun to laugh and play. When we were done, I told her that I needed to drop by my dad's house.

"Umm... I think it is way too soon to meet your father." Kasey exclaimed.

"He isn't there." I laughed because I could hear the sigh of relief. I hoped that one day they would meet. "I need to check the mail, feed the fish and we can get food there. He's away on business."

"I'm okay with that."

We reached my father's house. I guided Kasey by the hand to the living room. For the first time, we were in an indoor private space together. We kissed lightly on the lips before, but nothing more. There was an unexplainable energy growing so strong between us. I liked it and wanted to explore what it was. Before we could even get to the living room we stopped in the hall.

The sexual tension was obvious and mounting from the late-night conversations and time spent together. At this point, it was just a matter of time before something happened. I let the energy between us guide us to where we wanted to be. We were up against the wall passionately kissing, hands all over each other. I couldn't believe this woman was allowing this.

I stripped Kasey slowly, first taking her strap down on the right side as I kissed her neck, taking the other strap down and kissing her shoulder. I then gently unzipped her dress and kissed her right between her breasts. I continued kissing her sensually from the top of her head to her feet and then she took control. I found myself up against the wall. She pulled off my shirt, mimicking my moves, kissing my chest and lightly dragging her tongue down, stopping at my erection. She had me moaning, feeling good. I pulled her up gently before she could suck me dry. I was almost about to cum and wanted to collapse on the floor, but instead I walked her into the living room. I laid her down on the carpeted floor, head on a pillow. I gently positioned myself and I slid into her and we went at it slow and passionately. Damn this woman! I felt high and thankful my dad was away.

With her, time didn't matter. I don't know how long we made love for, or how long we laid on the floor afterwards. What I did know was we didn't have to rush to get up. My mind was all over the place with thoughts of what's next between us. I knew what I wanted, what I was thinking. I just hoped her thoughts were the same.

I guess our thoughts weren't on the same page in that moment because Kasey said, "I'm hungry."

"Let's see what we have in the fridge." I started to get up from the floor too when she asked a question.

"Can you show me the bathroom? I'd like to clean up." I could smell me all over her. I left myself with her, there were no barriers.

"Sure." I showed her the bathroom, while I went upstairs to clean up myself. As we rummaged for delectable food, I was worried that we moved too fast.

Kasey

I had no intentions of having sex with Justin that day. I was a tad excited and wanted to do it again. It just felt right. I was eating some chips and staring into space with nothing more than what had happened just a few minutes ago on my mind. It replayed slowly like a scene from a movie.

"Kasey, I hope you don't regret what just happened."

"Absolutely not. I was actually thinking about doing it again."

A huge grin came to Justin's face. "Delighted to hear that."

A thought crossed my mind that I just had to ask. "Please don't be offended, but when was the last time you were tested?"

"I had my physical about a month ago and I'm good. No partners since then. What about you? Are you on birth control?" Even though we were having this conversation after the fact, I felt it was necessary. We had talked about sex on the phone, but never about testing or birth control.

"I am on birth control and I go to the GYN in two weeks" I responded to Justin's question. "I tend to have irregular periods, which is originally why my doctor suggested birth control. I also had abnormal pap smears in the past." I wasn't worried about catching anything from Justin besides feelings and a new appetite for him. My last relationship was while in law school: a guy named Ryan. To be honest, Ryan couldn't hold a candle to Justin.

I picked up a picture off the coffee table. I could tell it was Justin's father.

"You look like your dad."

"I get that a lot." He retorted.

"I'm sure your son would come out looking exactly like the both of you."

"Let's bet on that."

"Seriously?"

"It's a bet I am willing to make." He said that as if we were going to have this baby together.

"You're on." I couldn't believe I bet on what his child would look like.

After we cleaned up from eating, we got in the car and he drove me home. Justin was holding my hand as he drove; I was falling asleep. When he pulled up to my building, he had to gently wake me, "you're home."

"Sorry I fell asleep."

"No worries. You looked so peaceful; I didn't want to wake you."

"Call me when you get in?"

"Yeah." Justin gave me a long passionate kiss. A kiss that said, *I would like to keep this going as long as possible*. Gently sucking on my bottom lip, tasting my tongue, gently and sweetly. When I got in, my house phone was ringing like crazy. It was just 9:30, but most people would call my cell. My mother probably. I prepared my mind for the conversation I was about to have. When I answered the phone and heard that it was Clarke (and not my mom), I instantly felt a wave of relief.

"Hey girl, where you been? I've been calling your cell and sending texts." That was when I remembered I had turned it off. I switched it back on and off it went. Voicemail, text, and other alerts sounded off.

"What's up Clarke?"

"You tell me. Who is he?"

"Who is what" I asked dismissively.

"Girl, don't play with me." Clarke was my best friend outside my family. Let's face it; there were some conversations you didn't have with your older brother. My god sister was the sister I never had. "Well, stop stalling."

"His name is Justin. We've gone out a few times, spoken every day in between dates. I really like him, but I don't want to rush into things."

"Kasey, have fun. Stop worrying. What time are you going to be over for the shower?"

"About 2."

"You know your mom is suspicious. You think you'll bring him to the wedding?"

I hadn't thought of that, whether I should've even asked him. Honestly, I felt it was too soon. I hadn't brought anyone around family since law school. Furthermore, I thought that meeting parents was reserved for people who you deemed to be highly important, someone you felt would be around for some time. "I am not sure about that."

"See how things play out," Clarke stated. She and I jabbered about wedding plans and shower/bachelorette fun before saying our goodbyes. I truly felt like she was my sister. As soon as I hung up. My cell went off. It was Justin. Immediately, I smiled.

"Hey, you home?" Justin asked.

"Yeah. I'm here. This afternoon was more than I could have hoped for."

"Me too. Justin, I'd like to cook dinner for you tomorrow night. I know you have to be up early, so if you can't, I understand."

"I'd love for you to cook for me. I can’t wait to taste you…I mean the food. I can’t wait to taste the food."

"Ha, is that right?" I giggled. Justin and I spoke for what seemed like such a short time, but in reality, it was an hour. We talked about our afternoon and our hopes for the future. Justin talked often about his grandmother with whom he was very close. She sounded like the epitome of strength. Surviving the segregated south, being widowed young, raising her children on her own. We said goodnight and he promised to be over by seven.

Justin

I could not wait for the day to be done. The weather was warming and the anticipation of seeing Kasey in her home was enough for me to get a hard on after yesterday. I got dressed and stopped to get a flower arrangement of calla lilies and something orange I didn't know the name of. I figured orange was her favorite color because her outfits always seemed to have a variation of the color. When I arrived, I began to feel my heart beating and palms sweating again. Damn this woman! She opened the door in a pair of jeans and a bright orange shirt. The smell was intoxicating. Scents of steak, rosemary and other spices I had no name for as they were mixed to create an aroma that made my mouth water. I gently kissed her on her lips, hungry for more but resisting. We walked into a beautiful sunken in one-bedroom apartment with walls covered in autumn colors, rich and warm. She had her degrees displayed, family photos covering the walls. Once I took a seat on the chocolate leather sofa, she handed me a glass of red wine, merlot.

"Dinner will be ready in a minute." Kasey sat on the other end of the sofa. Too far for my liking so I patted my hand on the sofa for her to come closer, which she did.

"Good. How was your day?" She leaned into me while I wrapped my arm around her shoulders.

"Pretty good. Sent a child home to his mother and hoping she continues to keep doing the right thing."

"I don't envy your work."

"If I don't do it, then who?"

"I suppose you're right."

"How was your day?"

"Typical. Work, then a workout. Relaxed until I came to see you."

We talked some more, then Kasey got up to check the food.

"Ready to eat?"

"Famished." I actually said grace out loud and she looked shocked. Not as shocked as I felt.

"I hope it was okay that I did that." I said hastily.

"It was perfect."

"I don't know what came over me. I don't usually pray out loud and well I don't really go to church either. Only with my grandma sometimes."

"I think that it was sweet. I go almost every Sunday. The way I was raised."

"I'd like to go with you if that's okay?"

"I think I would like that."

I took a sip of wine and asked, "Where did you buy this wine? I like it."

"Whole Foods wine shop on Columbus."

"I may have to stop in there at some point, pick this up and see what else they have."

"I usually go there or Trader Joes on 14th but, I honestly haven't been down that way in a while. I am usually riding past to work."

We continued to eat dinner and talk. The food was excellent. This woman was an athlete, could cook, was intelligent and, of course, gorgeous. I was getting used to this woman being in my life and I hoped she felt the same way.

Kasey

After dinner, we sat on the couch and sipped wine. I was getting wet with anticipation of experiencing of riding the wave again. Justin came closer and kissed me lightly on the lips. I returned the kiss with a hunger that I had never felt before. He began to undress me and went right to my warm essence. He hit the spot immediately and showed me that he knew his way around a woman's body. He licked and sucked and made me cum so hard. I cried! That never happened before. Wanting more, I took his hand, led him to my bedroom and took off the rest of my clothes. He undressed while we kissed, then I laid Justin down and slowly mounted him. I slid myself up and down his shaft which evoked a gutteral moan.

"Aaahhh!" I could see it was good to him so I started to go a tad faster.

"Aaahhh!" Justin was feeling it. I began to move even faster.

"Mmmm!" I rode for as long as he could take it. My breasts bouncing up and down as I took him in. Justin met my pace, driving himself into me until, finally, he erupted inside me.

"Aaahhh! Shit! Damn!" I slowly maneuvered off of him, kissed him like I wanted more. I went to the bathroom and came back with a warm washcloth to wipe off what he didn't leave inside me. This was the first man ever allowed to leave himself in me. My God, what was I doing? I laid my head on his chest and he stroked my head slowly.

"Kasey, are we moving too fast?"

"I feel like things are just happening. Not necessarily too fast. Are you enjoying it?"

"Yes."

"Like my god sis told me, let's just have fun."

We slept until his alarm started blaring from his phone. I gently roused him from sleep. "I hear it." Justin went to turn it off and got back in bed for what was too short of a time. I gave him a matching towel and washcloth, and he went to shower.

"Are you going back to sleep?" Justin asked.

"No, I'm up. Going to get a run in."

"Be careful. Text me later." We kissed and he left. I was so horny I couldn't focus to get my run clothes on. I broke out my pocket rocket and pleased myself with thoughts of Justin as his smell lingered on the pillow.

Justin

We had spent lots of time together over the last three weeks. Between the dates, visits to each other's homes, long and deep conversations I was ready to make the relationship official. We planned to go to church and brunch Sunday and I had made reservations for Calle Ocho.

Church was amazing. I felt different. I enjoyed the service and it was way better than my grandmother's. Felt more contemporary. The music was uplifting. I could relate to the message and for the first time in my life, I felt a sense of peace that I had never felt before. After leaving service, I was so nervous. Just like our first date. By the time we sat down, I was sweating, my hands were clammy and my mouth felt like the Sahara. Damn this woman!

"Jus, what's up?" Kasey inquired. "You've been acting strangely since we left church."

"I'm... well. Ummm." I tugged at my collar, unloosened my tie and the top two buttons of my shirt.

"Okay, you're starting to scare me a bit."

"I wanted to give you this." I reached into my pocket and gave her the gift. A charm bracelet. The charm was a double heart.

"Sweetie it's beautiful. What's the occasion?"

"I'm hoping that you will officially make our relationship exclusive."

"I would love that."

Kasey stood up and leaned over the table to kiss me. I cupped her face in my hands and sucked on her bottom lip. She pulled back to sit when the waiter arrived. I felt the third leg awaken. I sat back down and did all I could do to regain my thoughts. Finally, I was able to get control of my bodily functions. Damn This Woman!

"So, I've told you my god sister, Clarke is getting married in two weeks." Kasey said suddenly. "Will you go with me?"

"Yes, of course."

"My parents and brother will be there. The rehearsal dinner is Friday. I'd like you to come with. It is at Riverside Church and then dinner is at Londel's."

In my head that made me nervous, but then again it told me how serious Kasey was about our relationship. After brunch we went to a jazz lounge named Smoke. The music at was amazing. We listened and drank several rounds. She held my hand and I whispered into her ears.

On the way home, while driving, Kasey decides to test my control (or lack thereof) by giving me her best blow job performance. After about five blocks I had to make her stop.
It was dangerous. We stepped into my house and it was no holds barred. We couldn't get enough. That was when I knew. This was it. This was the woman I was supposed to be with. Sleep came upon us until her phone began to ring relentlessly. She went to find her purse to answer and I went to get a bottle of water.

"Hello mother." I heard Kasey say flatly. That was my cue to go to the bathroom and give her privacy. I could still hear her. "No, I'm not home." I got the impression that her mother was the overbearing type. "I know, I know. Mom, can we finish this tomorrow?" Kasey was obviously irritated. I wanted to fix that. "I will call you. I love you." Kasey was cute when she was frustrated. When she hung up, I gave a smirk.

"That woman drives me crazy."

"I see." I full out laughed at her.

"Babe, it's not funny."

I pulled her close. Kissed her lips. Kissed her neck. Picked her up, placing her on the counter. We kissed and I opened my robe she was wearing with a tug of the sash. I cupped her breasts and caressed her nipples before I pulled off my shorts. I slowly impaled her onto me and we ravaged each other right where we were, releasing tension and making each other feel like we were the only ones that mattered. Her moist vagina was warm and yet she was still nice and tight. Kasey was gorgeous and I realized, she would be a vision in white for me. Damn This Woman! She was changing me in so many ways. It was time for us to move forward, again.

I decided to take her to meet my grandmother.

"Where are we going?"

"You will see." We pulled up to the building, 145th and Lenox Avenue. It took a while to find a parking space, between the amount of buildings in the area and Mother Hale Bus Depot, we spent about twenty minutes driving around looking for a park. As we walked toward the building, I could see Kasey was immediately nervous.

"Is this your grandma's?"

"Yes."

"Oh. I... I..."

"You'll be fine."

"Is your dad here too?"

"I'm not sure. Haven't touched base with him this week." As we got off the elevator on the 12th floor and approached the apartment door the smell of good food was wafting into the hall. I rang the bell and my cousin, Kelly, answered the door. Before anything was said, my little cousin, Bryan, came running to the door.

"Justinnnnnnnnn!" I picked him up and he wrapped his arms around my neck and squeezed.

"Hey Bryan. How are you?"

"Good. Don't I get a dollar?"

"Let me see what I can do." We walked into the living room, Bryan on my hip.
"Bryan and Kelly, this is Kasey." Kasey went to extend her hand, but Kelly opened her arms to embrace her instead.

"I hope you don't mind. If he brought you to Nana's that means you are good people and he's into you." Kelly smiled at Kasey then at me. So far, so good.

Kasey

I couldn't believe I was meeting Justin's family. His cousin said what I was thinking when I realized I was meeting his Nana and family. Men don't go around taking girls that don't mean something to meet their family. After meeting Uncle Joe, we went into the kitchen and I was overwhelmed by all the food and dessert. There were two cakes on the counter one chocolate the other I was unsure of the flavor but the frosting was white with coconut shavings on top.

"Nana, this is Kasey." Justin stated proudly.

"Well my dear", Nana said warmly, it is lovely to meet you." She was a chocolate brown woman, with smooth skin, average height and medium framed.

"Same here. It smells wonderful. Can I help?"

"Yes. You sure can. You and Justin can start taking some of the food on that counter to the table."

"Yes Ma'am."

"Honey, I am Nana." I wasn't nervous anymore. They seem like down-to-earth loving people. I loved Nana's deep belly laugh. Bryan was a ball of energy, but he was sweet. He reminded me of my nephews. I was starting to feel comfortable around them.

Dinner was so good. Nana made baked chicken, macaroni and cheese, collard greens, homemade biscuits and iced tea. I was literally stuffed from the meal she prepared. She reminded

me of my grandma; I just loved her. She was warm and loving, welcoming and kind.
While we were eating, the doorbell rang. Kelly went to answer it. She returned with a man in tow and from the uncanny resemblance, I knew who he was.

"Dad."

"Hello everyone. Who do we have here?"

Bryan jumped in, "Justin's girlfriend. Ooooh."

Justin stood up to greet his father and to introduce me. "Boy, hush," he said to Bryan. "Dad this is Kasey." Placing his hand on my shoulder, I looked up at him as he gently squeezed it.

"Well it's nice to meet you, young lady." I turned to his dad, ready to stand to shake his hand, "No need to stand up, young lady. It's a pleasure to meet you. My son told me a lot about you. You must be something kind of special for Justin to talk about you the way he does." I could feel my cheeks get hot and I am sure they were visibly red from blushing.

"Nice to meet you too, sir."

I became nervous all over again. How much of me could Justin possibly had discussed with his father? I mean, we'd only been together for a little over a month. I couldn't dwell on it for too long as the dinner chatter continued as his father sat on the other end of the dining room table and joined in on the feast.

When it was time for dessert, I had eyes on Nana's coconut cake; I had asked Justin about it and he told me that once I tried a piece of it, I would never want anything else. Nana sliced into the cake cutting a nice size for me. Placing it on the plate, I was sure I drooled a bit. It had pineapple filling and a thick layer of frosting. It was so good and moist. And it was like a peace came over me! Pure comfort in each bite. It was *smack ya mama* good. Of course, I took some home to eat in the comfort of my pajamas.

Having dinner with Justin's family was a great way to end the weekend. Good people and good food. The dinner ended and we transitioned to the living room. There the conversation shifted to general talk to embarrassing events about Justin as a little boy and a teenager. To top it all off, there were photos shown of him when he had a flat top, oversized overalls and Cross Colours shirt in the eighth grade. He didn't enjoy the topic being about him nor pictures of his past being revealed to me either. Lucky for him, the night had come to an end, and we had to leave.

"Young lady, it was very nice meeting you." Justin's father said. "I am glad to see my son so happy."

"Thank you, sir, it was good to meet you too. You have a lovely family."
We hugged his family and parted for our drive back to his house. When we got in the car, Justin looked pretty happy.

"See, it wasn't bad at all, was it?" He asked me.

"Actually, it wasn't."

"As we were leaving, Nana said I could come by anytime. That was nice of her."

"She did, did she?" I was glad things went well and his family was so nice.

Two weeks later…

Up until this point, my life had been my family and work. Nothing else mattered much. You get to a point where you meet someone, and it just feels right. Things fit. A hand in a glove. Justin had my mind wondering things that I never had the opportunity to think of with a guy before: marriage, a house, and family.

The rehearsal dinner for Clarke and Jackson went off without a hitch. Justin met me at the restaurant. As always, he was looking quite sharp. His beard was fully grown out but, immaculately shaped. He kept his hair low and light. He wore his predictable going-out attire:

button up shirt, jeans and shoes. Someone was trying to impress the family.

I introduced Kyle and Lana, his wife, to Justin.

"Finally, nice to meet you." Justin reached for Kyle's hand and shook it.

"Same here. It seems like the two of you have been spending lots of time together."

"Kasey is very special to me." Drawing back his hand, Justin wrapped it around my waist.

"So, what are your plans for my sister?" I loved my brother. He asked questions and was very protective, but not a jerk about it. He was very much like my father, whom I loved so very much.

Before Justin could answer, I jumped in, "Okay, Kyle. Not today. We're here for Clarke. Let's talk futures later. Okay?" Kyle nodded his head and we all entered the room reserved for our party in the restaurant. I think I introduced Justin to everyone that meant a lot to me. He was now a major part of my life and I wanted everyone of importance to know him. Looking at him chat it up with my friends, I knew he would fit right into my life like the spot was made just for him.

When we got home, I couldn't wait to get Justin's clothes off. I had a few drinks with dinner and they had made my yoni wet and ready. This was a smash and grab. No chit chat, just taking what already belonged to me. Justin had me making all kinds of sounds that I didn't know were in me.

"Damn Babes."

"Yeah, I know."

After we came, we slept. I woke up very refreshed. So much so, that I sucked his dick awake and when it was at attention, I hopped on and rode Justin until he came.

The day of the wedding brought family, friends and acquaintances together to celebrate my god-sister. The day was beautiful for May; sun shining, but not killer hot.

"Sweets, you look fine, leave the make-up alone." I heard Justin say softly.

"I just want to be the perfect maid of honor and I am nervous about you meeting my mom. My dad, no problem, but my mom. She is just…"

"Gets under your skin."

"Yes, exactly." The church was beautiful. There were sprays of lilies and hydrangeas on the end of every other pew. At the front was an arch with all white roses and touches of baby blue roses for a pop of color. The sunlight was shining through the skylight. Clarke was gorgeous. At 5 feet 7 inches, she wore a beaded mermaid dress with a long train. Her makeup was au naturelle with brazen pink lip color and her hair was up in a perfect bun. Then I wondered what if, for myself. What if I got married? What would my wedding day look like?

"Kris, look at our girl. Gorgeous." I was loving my god-sis as a bride. She looked breathtaking.

"You are up next." Kristen said.

"Maybe one day."

The music started which signaled the arrival of Clarke. Everyone rose to their feet and turned toward the bride. Slowly, Clarke and her father walked down the aisle and we all choked up seeing her. Even Jackson, her new husband, couldn't hold back his tears. I got him a hankie with his initials embroidered on it. It was a small present I knew he would need. With all the tears and sniffling going on, I should have gotten a box of tissues for the entire bridal party.

During the cocktail hour, Justin officially met my parents.

"Mom, dad. This is Justin." I cautiously introduced him.

"Nice to meet you. I have heard good things about you." Dad, said.

"Sorry I can't say the same." My mother had to be snide. She turned her nose up to him as she looked away from him. Kyle was never good for support and laughed. He extended his hand to Justin. "Good to see you, again."

"Why has your brother met him and not us?" My mother started in again. Thankfully, my father immediately jumped in at that point.

"Ann, let's go say hello to some people. Son, it was nice to meet you." My dad was always helping put out mother's fires.

"Thanks a lot brother. You sure were helpful." I spat at Kyle.

"You should have given her something. She keeps calling asking why you have been MIA so much, plus I didn't tell her that I met him yesterday."

"You know why I don't say anything. If I do, she starts planning the rest of my life."

***

The reception was about to begin and I felt so nervous leaving Justin at the table with my parents, especially my mother. I had to give my toast to the bride and groom and for the first time in my life, instead of just a fleeting thought, I could picture getting married...to Justin that is.

"To my sister and friend Clarke and her new husband, Jackson, I pray that this journey brings you fun times and lots of love that bears good fruit. Hold on to one another when things are tough, communicate when the waters get rough, pray together, pray for one another and remember that together you can get through anything. I love you both."

The rest of the reception was lots of dancing and saying hello to familiar faces. I was so happy to spend time with my girls. It had been a little while since we all hung out, except the wedding planning, bachelorette party and bridal shower.

“Kristen, we have to get together more often," I said.

“Yes. Especially now all this wedding business is done with Clarke."

“I see you got rid of crazy Karen.”

“I got rid of her, but she didn't quite get rid of me." Clarke rolled up on us. "What are you two discussing?"

"Krissy's crazy ass ex." I replied.

"Sarah seems nice, you should keep her. Especially since she is working you over," Clarke said.

"Very funny. Karen keeps calling, texting and stalking." I was worried about my girl after what she just said. She needed an Order of Protection. We kept chatting until Clarke got swept away from us. Then we all went back to dancing.

Krissy's girl had some moves. Kind of impressed. Kris and her new girl were showing off and having a good time.

The reception ended and my mother sure was not letting me get away without one last comment.

"Kasey, please call me tomorrow so we can set up a time for you and Justin to have dinner at the house. Since you are parading him at a wedding, I'd like to know more about him." She spoke as if he wasn't even standing there.

"ill do. Love you both." I said quickly. My father shook Justin's hand, kissed my cheek and said goodbye. We got in the car. I was exhausted.

"That was nice," Justin said, "thanks for inviting me."

"Even my mother's behavior?" I replied.

"It was fine. You are more like her then you care to admit."

I was seething mad from that comment. I never want to be like that woman. Ever! I love my mother but she is so... I couldn't even find the words. "That was cold."

Justin

After the wedding we agreed to meet Kasey's parents for Sunday dinner the following week. Their home was beautiful: six bedrooms, antique furnishings, beautiful backyard. We ate dinner on the deck. I really liked Kasey's dad. He was a sports buff, just like me.

"I play touch football on the weekends. I love it." I told Kasey's father.

"Where are the games?"

"Randall's Island."

"May come check you out."

"I would like that, sir."

While Kasey was helping her mom in the kitchen, her dad and I continued to talk about my time in college, my previous marriage and the reason I ended up working in sanitation. When the meal was complete, the blessing was said and we ate. I was waiting for the firing squad. I seem to have connected with her father; her mother was altogether different. It felt as if she was looking for fault.

"Justin, what are your intentions with my daughter?" Kasey's mom said suddenly.

I nearly choked on a fork full of salad. Who says that? I felt like I was in the 1950's and meeting her father for the first time.

"Ann, let the man eat in peace." Kasey's father tried to defuse the situation.

"Well James, I just want to know what kind of man my daughter has been keeping company with and where he sees the relationship going."

"Mom, that is not all on Justin. I do get a say, you know." Kasey tried to save me. Unfortunately, her mom was relentless.

"Of course, you do. What is it that you do again?"

"I work full time for sanitation." I could see where this line of questioning was going and it was pissing me off. People made all kinds of assumptions about me because I hauled garbage for a living. Was I passionate about it? No. However, it paid my bills and the benefits were great. I also did get a degree in economics and an MBA. I did a five-year dual degree program.

"Oh, sanitation. You haul garbage for a living? Ay Dios mio, my daughter is dating the trashman."

"Mom, that is rude and this isn't a job interview." Kasey responded.

"Ann, do keep in mind that your parents were not a fan of me when we first started dating." Kasey's dad was definitely the more levelheaded of the two. I wondered how he dealt with Kasey's mom.

"My grandparents were not happy that my mom had taken up with a negro." Now I began to understand a bit better the behavior I was receiving from Kasey's mother.

Kasey's dad was unaffected. "Yes, I was negro, dark skinned, American and lazy and they did not want me with their daughter. In time, that changed."

We continued to talk through the meal and when we left, Mr. Walker shook my hand. It assured me that he was okay with my relationship with his daughter. On the ride home, I guess I was a tad tense. The conversation with Kasey's mom did not sit well with me. Frankly, I was still pissed off. The ride was quiet because I didn't have anything to say. I was in my head replaying the conversation at dinner. Kasey was falling asleep as she often does in the car. There was no traffic and we got to her house in no time.

"Are you staying with me tonight?", Kasey said.

"Nah. I am going to go home."

"Jus, is everything okay? I apologize about my mother's behavior."

"It's fine."

"No, it isn't. She thinks she has the right to choose for me."

"Kasey, stop it. I don't want to have this conversation. Let it be before we say things we don't mean. End of discussion! I will call you when

I get in." I know my tone was harsh and this had turned into something unnecessary, but I needed to be alone with my thoughts. It's hard when you have an education but your actual occupation doesn't add up. Going to college was great, but finding employment after was more difficult. When I got in, I called as I promised, but got no answer. I decided to let things be for the night.

Kasey

I didn't want to answer when he called. I was being stubborn. I was angry and hurt by the tone he used during our last conversation. I was also angry that my mother may have messed things up for me and my new relationship. Why did my mother feel like she had the right to say and do whatever she felt like? Why did he think he could talk to me like that? This was the first time ever he spoke to me in that way. I loved this man, but how do I make her understand? I called my brother because he understood.

A familiar voice answered although, it wasn't Kyle's. "Hello."

"Hi Lana, I hope I didn't wake you." I should have called his cell.

"No, I'm up. You want to speak to Kyle?"

"Yes please." I could overhear her in the background telling Kyle I sounded upset.

"Hey Sis, what did she say?"

"She was so judgmental. She basically insulted the work he does, allowing it to overshadow who he is and what he has accomplished. It was worse than when Lana met her."

"Is that even possible?"

"Brother, I tell you it is. She is crazy."

"What did dad say?"

"He did what he always does. Tried to get her to stop and acknowledge that abuelo and abuela didn't like him. The worst part is that we got into it on the way home. Now I feel bad and you know me."

"Do you care for him?"

"Yes."

"Give him time. I love you and support you."

"Love you too. Tell Lana goodnight."

I still didn't want to call Justin. Maybe tomorrow. Tomorrow had come, three times over. It was now Wednesday and I had not heard from him and I didn't call either. I guess our true colors were showing. I knew he was okay because his posts were showing up in my news feed.

One should never allow another person's opinion to dictate their feelings for a loved one.

Maybe I was reading into it, but it felt as if he was referencing our relationship. I think that made me more frustrated. Speak to me directly, not through subliminal messages on social media. I was at work outside the courtroom speaking with a co-worker and all of a sudden, I felt nauseated. I chalked it up to eating lunch too fast. By the days end, I was wiped out. When I got in, I called Clarke to see how her honeymoon was. I had not spoken to her since her return.

"Welcome back, how was it?"

"Dreamy and lots of fun. I didn't want to return home." It sounded as Clarke was still on a honeymoon high.

"I can imagine."

"How are you?"

"Good. Tired from work. Had a tough case with a three-year old. I'm trying to put it out of my mind."

"That, I don't want to imagine. How's Justin?" The dreaded question. I didn't really want to rehash the whole thing.

I simply said, "He's fine."

"The four of us should do brunch."

"Let me talk to him about that." We talked more about the wedding and how we should ask Krissy and her new girlfriend to join us for brunch, then hung up. I most certainly did not hear from Justin that night. I didn't call him either.

The next morning, I checked my cell. Nothing. I did my normal morning routine: run at 5am, shower and dress, eat breakfast. Right before I was about to walk out the door, I had to race to the bathroom. I vomited. I felt awful. Somehow, I pulled it together and got out the house. The train ride this day was awful. The smells were hitting my nose and making me feel worse. I made it through the morning on seltzer and ginger cookies. I had a salad for lunch and about fifteen minutes later, was in the bathroom. I thought maybe I had the stomach flu. There was no fever. When I reached home, I just crawled into bed. I was so tired lately. Too tired to swim or run. The rest of the week was more of the same. Saturday, I woke up feeling a little bit better. Had a slice of toast with peanut butter. Waited fifteen minutes to see if it would stay down. It did. I went for an early morning run. Of course, I went down the west side highway. On my way back, I hoped to see him and I didn't. The next week, the girls and I decided to hang out after work. We met at Verlaine. The lychee martinis were superb. Of course, Krissy was late. We all chit chatted on the things happening in our lives. I had half a martini and made a b-line to the bathroom. The one upstairs was not occupied. I would not have made it downstairs. When I returned, Clarke shot me a look.

"What?" I said.

"How long has this been happening?" Clarke says.

"About two weeks."

Krissy chimes in, "You took a test yet?"

"Test for what?"

"Silly...a pregnancy test."

"No. I can't be. You two are talking crazy."

Clarke always was one to take charge. "Let's go. We are getting the check."

We went to my house after buying a box of three home pregnancy tests. We skipped the long train ride and took an Uber. It never dawned on me that I could be pregnant. I had irregular periods and... maybe I forgot a few times to take my pill. The lines showed immediately. It was positive. I began to sob.

"I know this isn't what you expected, but you can provide a good life for this baby." Clarke said.

"It isn't that. Justin and I haven't been speaking since we visited my parents."

"That was weeks ago." Krissy said.

"You have to tell him,." Clarke said.

"She's right, he has a right to know." Krissy said.

They started squealing. Awwwww, Kasey's going to be a momma! Then I realized, forget Justin... Who was telling my parents? The girls left with a warning that I had better call the doctor to make an appointment. I needed to sleep in the next day. I was so tired. My thoughts raced. Finally, I opened my eyes. How was I going to tell my parents? How was I going to tell Justin? Was he going to be part of the baby's life? What would happen if he didn't? I just started this job. How would I care for this baby and continue my career? My early morning thoughts were interrupted by my phone ringing. It was Kyle.

I answered wearily. "Hey Kyle."

"Are you in bed still?"

"Yes, I'm feeling a little sick."

"I'll be in town for about a week with Lana and the kids. You sure you don't want me to call mom?"

"No, please don't call mom. I'll be fine. See you soon. Love you."

I needed to go to the doctor and give myself time to get better. I also didn't want him asking about Justin.

Justin

I had not seen Kasey or heard from her in about two to three weeks. It was a trying time. I was in my head. I missed the time I spent with Kasey. I had gotten used to being with her on a regular basis, waking up to her beautiful face. Let's face it, I was in love. I hoped that she would call but, I was just as guilty. I spent most of the time working, working out and waiting. I had gone to church with my grandmother and she made Sunday dinner.

"Son, where is Kasey?" Nana asked.

"I don't know Nana."

"Something wrong?"

"Nana, we got into it and it's been weeks since I've heard from her. We got into an argument after visiting her parents. I didn't like what her mother said about me working for sanitation. I also felt insecure, like I wasn't good enough. I yelled at Kasey. I know I was wrong, but..." Nana cut me off.

"Did you call and apologize?"

"No."

"Well, call. You look like you lost your dog. Swallow your pride and if you really care, call. Son, there is nothing worse than a person who can't admit when they're wrong. If this relationship is exciting and scary that probably means it is the one you should fight for. You should make amends. It's obvious that you love her."

I left my Nana's and got in the car. Pressed the voice dial. "Kasey." The phone rang and finally, the voice I longed to hear came booming through my car.

"Hello."

"Hey Sweets. You sound like you were asleep."

"Justin. Thought you forgot about me."

"Sweets, I'm coming over to talk face to face, if that's okay..."

"It's fine."

"See you in fifteen." The butterflies returned. I was so excited to see her. I missed her. Wasn't sure of what to say, except to apologize. Would she even accept my apology? I needed her to know that I loved her and I wouldn't let anything else come between us moving forward. She opened the door, beautiful as ever. Even in sweats, no makeup and looking like she just woke up. I kissed her on the cheek and we sat at the table.

"You're sipping ginger tea. Are you sick?"

Kasey hesitated before she answered. "I'm going to the doctor in the morning."

"You need me to come with?"

"I can go alone."

"Just offering. I miss you. I'm sorry I didn't call, it was wrong."

Kasey excused herself and went to the bathroom but, the one in her bedroom. Something was different. It was like she lost weight. When she came back, I asked, "Sweets, what's going on? You look sick and you are not telling me. I know we haven't spoken and I take responsibility for that but..." She stopped me.

"Justin, I'm glad you came over and I'm glad we have mended fences. I'm fine."

We talked for about an hour.

"Kasey, I want to apologize for the night in the car. I was wrong to speak to you like that. I also should have called sooner. I allowed my pride to get in the way of how I really feel."

"I appreciate your apology. I missed you and was hurt that you didn't call sooner. I honestly wasn't sure what to think."

"In the future, I will make sure that I communicate how I am feeling and not just cut you off."

"I would appreciate that."

During the conversation she made several trips to the bathroom. The last time, I followed her. She was vomiting.

"Get out of here, Justin."

"I can handle you vomiting."

I took the washcloth and ran cold water over it and put it on the back of her neck after she sat on the toilet.

"Please tell me, how long has this been happening, Kasey?"

"Just a few days. I told you, I am going to the doctor in the morning."

"I think it is best that you lay down. I am going to go and call me after your appointment." I pulled the covers up over her and took the spare keys locking the door behind me.

I always called my Nana when things troubled me. My dad was good for man to man conversations, but heart to hearts were reserved for Jessie Mae. I pushed the voice dial button.

"Nana."

"Hey son, did you talk to her?"

"Yes, but something is off. I don't know what, but she looks like she has lost weight and she kept running to the bathroom. The last time I followed behind her and she was vomiting. I'm worried."

"Son, sounds like you are in love."

"I do love her, but I've never been able to say it. After we got in that fight, it made it clear that she was in my heart."

"Son, let it rest for this evening and call her tomorrow."

That night I couldn't sleep. I had so many thoughts in my head. I hoped that she just had a stomach bug, nothing too serious. I was so tired at work but I got through the day. I texted her to see how her appointment had gone and she didn't respond. I called twice but she didn't answer. I decided to just go by the house and check in on her. I used the spare key. I found her asleep on the couch. I left her there and made dinner. I think the smell of lamb woke her.

"Sweets, you're up" I said softly.

"How long have you been here?"

"A few hours."

"What is that smell?"

"Lamb. You hungry?"

"I guess." We sat at the table and she looked so drained.

"Sweets, what did the doctor say?" She started to cry and now I was afraid of what she would say. I go to her. "Sweets, talk to me. What happened at the doctor?"

"I went to the GYN and..." Kasey was crying and rubbing her hands together. I tried to stay calm. I was thinking the worst, especially because of the weight loss. She had abnormal pap smears and I just knew I was about to hear that she had cancer that had spread. My mind was going in so many directions.

"Justin, I'm pregnant and it's twins." I was stunned. My mind didn't fully process the information.

"Justin, did you hear me?"

I think I heard her say twins. Babies. She's pregnant. How did this happen? I mean, I know how it happened. One baby...okay, but two at once? This cannot be happening.

"Yes baby, I heard you. I thought you were on the pill. I just don't understand."

"I was. Are you angry? I mean, there were days I forgot to take it. I should have been better about that. "

"You forgot?"

"I said I'm sorry. Look, if you don't want to be part of this I guess, I understand. I have already processed how I may have to be a single parent."

"What? How could you even think that?"

"We haven't spoken in about three weeks after our first real argument. I didn't think I would hear from you."

"So, if I didn't call or come by, you weren't going to tell me." I was feeling irritated. For her to even think that I would have children and she wouldn't tell me. I had to calm down.

"I planned to but, as you can see, I've been pretty sick."

"Kasey, even if we decided not to be together, I would never abandon my children. I want us to be together, that's why I called and apologized. I realized how my lack of action would make it harder and I didn't want any more time to pass. I am going to be a father. Daddy. Dad. Pop. A father."

I picked Kasey up, hugged and kissed her. I couldn't explain how happy I was. So many things were in my head.

"Sweets, who else knows?"

"Just the girls know I'm pregnant, but they don't know it's two babies."

"Two babies? Are you sure?"

"Yes."

"We're having twins. WOW! How come you look like your losing weight?"

"Because I've been having trouble keeping food down. The doctor said at my next visit, if it doesn't get better, then I may have to be admitted to the hospital. It is called hyperemesis gravidarum. I'm scared."

"Sweets, it will be fine. I'm here. What else did the doctor say?"

"He said they look fine. He told me to eat as healthy as possible, continue to take prenatal vitamins. I am already eight weeks. Swimming is fine but no running or triathlon. If the nausea and vomiting persist call him or just go to the hospital."

"When can we tell people?"

"I want to wait for another a month."

"Nana is going to be thrilled." Kasey started crying again. "Why are you crying?"

"My parents. Who is going to tell them?"

"We will tell them together." I refused to leave her that night. We went to bed and she fell out immediately. I was so excited that I couldn't sleep. Time had moved fairly quickly and I spent all my time at her house. The only time I seemed to be home was to switch out clothes. We needed to talk about living arrangements.

Kasey

Justin was so excited. I was happy that he shared my enthusiasm. I hoped that things would change now that I was in my second trimester. I was showing quite a bit and had to readjust my wardrobe recently. In the past few days my food was staying down, most of the time. I had only gained back three pounds of what I lost. It was time to tell my parents. We were going to their house for Labor Day. Kyle, Lana and the kids would also be there. I could tell them all at once. We took a drive up to my parent's house. While in the car, I was so nervous.

"Sweets, I think we need to figure out our living arrangements."

"What do you mean?"

"Well I'm always over at your house and that is going to increase. Your apartment is not big enough for three additions. I would like us to buy a home."

"You really have been thinking about this?"

"Absolutely. I want us to be a family."

"I love you!"

"Love you back, Sweets."

We arrived at my parent's house and apparently there were some other guests I didn't expect. My mother was being her usual self. I played with my nephews and got excited because I'd be giving them cousins. They were growing so quickly. I wished my nephews lived closer.

My mother broke me out of my private thoughts with a brash comment about my clothing. "That dress does nothing for your shape."

"Mom, back off."

"Excuse me, I am the mother here."

"Yes, yes you are but, I can't deal with negative criticism today." Justin came over and my mother walked away. This was not going the way I had planned. This woman tried my patience and then the tears started flowing. Why was I crying now? Why were my hormones getting the better of me today? Justin and I went inside to my old bedroom.

"I want to show you something. I pulled out my old diary from a box in the closet.

"Sweets, you want to go?"

"No, she isn't the only reason I'm here. Look at this."

"Your old diary."

"Yep, by the time I was writing in this one, I was in about 11th or 12th grade. There is something in particular I want to find." Flipping through the pages I found it. I read it aloud.

"When I get older, I hope to find a man who loves me. Someone who will be like my dad. Protective. Strong. Loving. Kind. I closed it. I am glad I found you Justin. You are all those things."

"Thanks Sweets. Are you sure you want to stay?"

"Yes. I'm fine now."

"So, how many boys have you brought in here before?"

"You are the first."

"Lies you tell." We cracked up laughing as he held me.

We went back on the deck and Kyle was handing me a cup with some alcoholic concoction in it. The smell alone was turning my stomach. "No thanks."

"You're turning down my rum punch? What's the matter with you?" Lana gave me a look that said *I know*. She had great instincts and proved to be a good sister-in-law. At that point, I knew I had to say something and since it was only Justin, Kyle, Lana and I on the deck, I did.

"Justin and I are having twins."

Kyle had a smile of excitement. He shook Justin's hand and gave him a brotherly hug. Lana hugged and kissed me and said, "Two babies?"

"Yep, two."

"When are you telling your parents?" She said.

"We are supposed to tell them today however, after the scene earlier, I'm getting cold feet."

"Stay strong, the three of us got your back." When most of the food was done, my dad said a blessing and I felt like I had not eaten in years. I had chicken, pulled pork, rice and beans, pasta salad, garden salad and a turkey burger. I stayed away from the hot dogs although, I wanted one. My mom had lots of desserts to eat too. I was making up for the three almost four months of regurgitating everything. She must have noticed because she started in.

"Kasey, you may want to slow down. You look like a pig in the trough."

I took a deep breath. "Look, I'm tired of your negativity, disregard for my feelings and overall nasty attitude."

"Who do you think you are talking to?" I've never seen my mother act so incredulous.

"You! That's who. No one wants to be abused and ridiculed constantly, especially by someone who is supposed to love them. Why can't you just love me for who I am?" By this time, Justin, Kyle and dad had come closer to the conversation, I guess to remind us of the guests that weren't family. That didn't stop my mom though.

"Te crié para ser el mejor y estar con el mejor. Podrías haber trabajado en muchos lugares, pero trabajas con esas personas. Saliendo con un hombre de la basura." My mother is crazy. She had the audacity to say, "I *raised you to be the best and with the best. You could have worked in many places. Instead you work with those people. Dating a garbage man."*

"Honestly, this is not the life I wanted for you. You were supposed to work in a top law firm, marry someone of stature and instead you're dating a garbage man. A GARBAGE MAN! Ay Dios Mio."

"You clearly have no idea about who I am and have become," I spat back. "I am exactly who you raised me to be. An independent woman who looks to find the best in people. I have found a loving man who respects me. Until you apologize, don't speak to me."

Kyle tried to pull me away and Justin too. By this time, the tears had started again and I was getting that feeling that the food may not stay down.

"Justin loves me and I love him and he isn't going anywhere. You had better get used to his presence because I'm having his babies." She looked at me and at him.

"You are going to what?"

"Yes, having his children."

"You are going to have the trash man's children?"

"Don't say it again. You are rude, disrespectful and miserable."

"Whoa! Whoa!" Justin was stunned by her comments. I know there's much he wanted to say but wouldn't out of respect for me, not her.

"Sweets, I think I am going to wait outside, by the car." I could feel the steam coming off of him as he rushed out the door. I stopped crying long enough to say goodbye to my family. My dad came to speak to me as I walked toward the car.

"Sweetie, please know that she just wants the best for you."

"Dad, she is mean. She says things without thinking about the impact it has on other people. It is wrong."

"I am not saying she is right. She is still your mother. Give her time."

"Dad, I don't know."

"Well, I am very excited." My dad was thrilled by the news. That was enough for me. After saying goodbye to the other family members. My dad walked me to the car and gave Justin and I his blessing.

"Justin, take care of my baby and her babies. I wish you two were married but, everything in time."

"Sir, this was not how I intended this to happen. Once things are all in place. I will marry your daughter."

"Justin, I know you love her."

"Love you, Daddy."

"Sugar Plum, I love you too. Give your mother some time."

We drove home. *Summertime* by Fresh Prince and Jazzy Jeff blared from the speakers. The summertime was my favorite. Barbeques, fresh fruit and, as I got older, making drinks with Kyle. This song brought back good vibes and memories. Before my mother became so critical of who I was. It was only 5pm, but it felt like 10pm. I attempted to use the voice dialing. I pushed the button. "Nana." The voice dialing only seemed to work for him. Justin laughed at me. I glared at him. "Not funny J, can you call her. I want to go over."

Justin

After Kasey and I told Nana about the pregnancy, they talked more than Nana and I did. I loved that they had their own relationship. Kasey only knew her maternal grandparents and that was for a short time. I think her relationship with Nana filled that void, even at our age. Nana was eager to see us and of course, ready to feed us.

"Nana, we just ate. Who did you cook all this food for?" I was full although, my nose was assaulted by good smells. Chopped BBQ, chicken, black eyed peas, cabbage, cakes and more cakes.

"Your dad said he was coming by, Uncle Joe, Kelly and Bryan. They went out for a bit but, they will be back. Honey, what's the matter?" She said to Kasey. I guess Kasey was still thinking about her argument with her mother and was wearing her emotions on her sleeves.
Before she could get any words out, she cried. More tears streaming down her face.

"Kasey, are the babies okay?" Nana said.

"Yes, ma'am. Nana, I've done pretty well for myself. I finished school, I work, I haven't gotten into any trouble. Why can't my mother just be proud of me and let me be?"

"She loves you."

I let them talk and watched TV until my dad showed up. I told him we were having twins and he cried and told me how happy and proud my mother would have been. That hit me in a place I wasn't prepared to go. I wish my mother and the woman carrying my children could have met. I missed my mother. Sometimes it felt like the memories were fading, but she remained in my heart. Dad asked if I thought about marriage. I had been thinking that since the first time I brought her over. I actually bought a ring shortly after I found out she was pregnant. I just didn't know when the right time was to ask. Our focus was on the babies.

We got home and crashed after that long day. She looked beautiful. I woke up to Kasey in a pale pink nighty that showed off her budding baby bump. She pulled my legs to the edge of the bed, placed a pillow on the floor and sucked my manhood until it was at full attention. She laid me down and slowly rode me. I watched as her vagina covered and uncovered my shaft repeatedly. Her breasts bounced as she moved up and down creating a rhythm that was oh so familiar. She was so wet. I felt like she would slide right off. I pushed all thoughts of being scared of intercourse to the back of my mind. She rode me until I came. That was some of the best sex I'd ever had. It was nice to be inside her again after such a long time. We lay together. Held one another. She was my Queen.

***

"I called a friend of mine and he has a few houses to show us." I said to Kasey.

"Really? Where?"
She sounded enthused. That's when a familiar feeling came back. Knots in the pit of my stomach, sweaty palms and heart palpitations.

"Well, where is it? I know that look. You're nervous. Spill it!"

"One is in Yonkers." I was stalling. I had to tell her that the better home was close to her parents. She would love to be close to her dad, but, her mother… well, they weren't speaking. I had hoped they would move past their differences. They are both so stubborn.

"Well, the other house is where?"

"White Plains."

"You're kidding, right?"

"No, he found a nice 4-bedroom house with a completed basement apartment. The school district is great and we can still commute to the city." She didn't respond to my sell. I just hoped that in the next few days she would at least go see it.

Kasey

The day had come where I had no choice but, to go see the houses. I pouted all the way. I did not want to live close to my mom. Justin had good points about the neighborhood. He had me get dressed up because we were going to dinner after. He would not say where though. We drove up to the house. The realtor was there waiting. I realized

Justin pays close attention. It was a home I had loved since childhood. The few times we had been up here to visit my parents I pointed it out and he remembered. We walked around the two-story home. Leaves were turning brown. Nice fall scenery flanked the home. The current owners set up was beautiful, of course I'd make my own changes. Add my own flare. Was I really considering this home? Living closer to my mother?

"What do you think?"

"I love it!"

"But."

"No but, I love it."

"Will you consider it? I know it is close to your parents--"

I cut him off. "I can't worry about that, this is about us, our children and future. I will look at the other options, but this is my first choice."

We left that home to view two others. The second one was nice however; the basement was unfinished and I just wasn't feeling it. The third was a huge fixer upper. We neither had the funds or the time for that. It was about 4pm when we were done. We got in the car and chatted about what we saw. I fell asleep as I often do. When I woke up, we were by Chelsea Piers.

"Where are we going?" Justin just smiled. When we got out of the car it was obvious, we were at Pier 61 and going on a boat ride. I was excited to be going on a dinner cruise.

"This is awesome. What's the occasion?"

"Wanted to celebrate us building our lives together."

"Babe, I love you."

"And I you."

Justin

She had no idea that the entire family was aboard the boat. The house shopping helped to distract her from the plans I was making with Clarke. I couldn't wait to propose. Would she say yes? I would be so embarrassed if her response was no in front of her family. It was way too late for these thoughts. I needed to breathe because I was having familiar feelings of nervousness like our first date. When we got on the boat, the music was already going. Pregnant and all, Kasey wanted to two- step. We were having a great time and she was singing *Before I Let Go* while dancing.

"Babes, you having fun?"

"Justin, yes. This was a great idea. I do think I need some water." I went to get the water and Kasey kept dancing. I was still nervous and hopeful. I thought about my mother and hoped she was looking down on this moment proud of me and the maturity that had taken place over the years.

My dad was by the bar. "Son, you ready?"

“Dad, I am so nervous. My mouth feels like cotton.”

He handed me his drink and said, “Sip to take the edge off.” After sipping what I knew was Macallan twenty-five neat, I felt relaxed.

Son, you got this, I heard my dad say as I walked back toward the dance floor. Kasey did a slight spin and ended up facing me. Then she spotted Clarke and Jackson behind me.

"Clarke."

"Hey girl. You looked good out there."

"What are you doing here?" Before Clarke could answer Kasey spotted her brother and parents. “Justin what is everyone doing here?"

I got down on one knee. My grandmother, father, Uncle Joe and cousin, Kelly were there too. She started tearing up.

"Kasey, you know I love you. I want to continue to show my love by asking you to be my wife, allowing me to be your life partner, friend, companion, protector, the father of your children, your husband. Will you marry me?"

With tears in her eyes Kasey said yes. "Yes, yes I will."

I put the ring I had been hiding for weeks on her finger. While the crowd clapped and cheered, her dad and brother came to shake my hand. Her friends were all cooing over her and the ring. It was a beautiful moment. We danced until her feet hurt.

"Justin, this was an amazing night. I had a great time." I was going to be a husband and father. This brought joy and pride to my heart. This time I was more prepared to take on these roles. This time I felt more secure in my life and self.

***

In the middle of the night. The phone rang.

"Hey dad."

"Justin, I need you to come to St. Luke's Hospital." It was my Nana's voice.

"Nana, what's wrong?"

"It's your dad. They think it was a heart attack." I was on autopilot from the time I hung up until we arrived at the hospital. Kasey would not allow me to leave her behind. He was rushed into bypass surgery.

That car ride as short as it was felt like the longest ride ever. I was not ready to be orphaned. Losing one parent is hard. To lose another, I wasn't ready for this. Especially the parent I spent the most time with. Sometimes, memories of my mother aren't so clear. I didn't want to lose my father and so close to the babies coming. I said a prayer as Kasey held my hand. The doctor came out to speak to us after which felt like an eternity. He said dad had a long road to recovery, but the surgery went well.

"When can we see him?" I said.

"I suggest you all go home, rest and come again in the morning. He is still heavily sedated." The doctor replied.

"I just want to see him and I'll go." I said.

The doctor agreed to let Nana and I go in. We stayed for about five minutes. I had never seen my dad look so vulnerable. The last time I had these feelings was at the loss of my mother.

I said a prayer. "God, please allow my father to heal. Give him strength and hope to work back to health. Allow us as a family to be strong and rally around him. Lord, we know that you do all things well and we pray for your continued blessings. Allow my father to meet my babies. Lord we love you and thank you. Amen."

"Amen, son. Amen" Nana joined in.

"Nana, he can't go. I'm just not ready."

We left the hospital, all pretty somber. We dropped Nana home and Kasey and I went home as well.

It was unnerving. How could one of the best nights of my life turn so quickly? We got home and crashed.

The next morning, Kasey slept in. It took a lot of convincing to get her to rest. She said she would Uber over in a few hours. I woke up, showered and rushed out to see dad at the hospital. The only thing on my mind was, get there so I'd know he was okay with my own eyes. I had not spoken to anyone and honestly didn't want to. When I arrived, Nana was already there. Dad was awake. As I stepped into the room, I remembered all the things I learned from my father. How to ride a bike, how to drive, the conversations about girls and sex, the conversation about being a black man in America. It was just he and I for so long. The day my mother passed. He said, there were things only my mother could teach me and there were things that only he could teach me. Then he said, "we'll figure this out together. It's me and you from now on."

"Hey dad."

"Justin, how are you?"

"Shouldn't I be asking you that?" We chuckled.

"Dad seriously, how are you?"

"In some pain, but I will be okay."

"You had me on edge." I felt choked up. I didn't want to lose my father. He taught me to be a man. Let's face it, I didn't want to be orphaned and all my selfishness came to the surface. I wanted him here to meet his grandchildren and see me marry Kasey. I was glad to see with my own eyes that he was a bit better. God heard my prayers for healing.

I silently said, “thank you.”

Kasey

I woke up knowing Justin had left out and I was alone with my thoughts. What a night of highs and lows. I was worried about his dad, but excited! Babies and a husband. Then my phone rang, breaking my focus on the things to come. I looked at my screen and saw that it was my mother.

"Hello."

"Kasey, I was calling to find out how Justin's father was doing." My mother was amazing. She has not spoken to me since Labor Day and here it is October and she is calling to inquire about my fiancé’s father. She barely said anything to me last night. Not even congratulations. What part of the game is this? I didn’t understand.

I decided just to answer. "He came out of surgery okay. He still has a long road to recovery."

"That's good to hear. Well I will speak to you soon." She hung up! I couldn't believe her. She didn't ask how I or the babies were doing. This woman was ... I couldn’t even find the words to describe her. I needed to speak to Kyle. I dialed. It rang. He answered.

"Hey what's up?"

"Kyle, your mother is crazy!"

"I need you to calm down before those babies come sooner than we would like." I took a deep breath.

"Brother, I swear she's nuts. She calls, asks about Justin's dad and hangs up."

"Oh, you were who she was going on about."

"What do you mean?"

"I saw her on the phone and when she got off, she was mumbling in Spanish. I figured whoever it was she was pissed at them."

"Why is she upset with me? I'm her daughter. She stopped talking to me."

"You both are so stubborn. She was attempting in her own way to make amends. Her pride is getting in the way. She asks what is going on with you all the time. I will admit, I have told her that you are well. I'm sure most of the details about the pregnancy comes from Dad."

"Lord. That woman is a maniac."

"You are going to have to be the bigger person here."

"No, no, no! I refuse." I was having my own tantrum.

Kyle was trying to be slick, playing on my emotions. I refused to give in to this. I got showered and made my way to the hospital to support my fiancé. I liked how that sounded. When I arrived to my future father-in-law's room, the mood was somber. Apparently, he took a dive for the worst. I walked over to his bedside and held his hand and Justin stood behind me and we prayed for healing.

"Sweets, I want you to go home and rest."

"I'm fine. I promise."

"Well, have you eaten?"

"I had something before I left."

"Did it stay down?"

"Will you leave her be. I'm sure if something was off, she would tell you." Nana swatted at him.

"Thanks Nana."

"I think Nana and Kelly need some food." I said.

"Kasey, fine, let's go and bring something back." Justin said. It was hard to see him so upset and frustrated.

My phone vibrated in my purse. I fished it out to see an unexpected caller.

"Good Morning, Kasey speaking."

It was the realtor. Letting us know that the offer we made was being considered and we should have a go on Monday to move forward. Buying a home was a long and arduous process.

Justin

My dad wasn't the person I knew before my mom passed. He seemed to always be on the go, most of the time with me in tow as long as it did not interfere with my education. I guess he missed his wife and companion more than ever. My father dated but he never remarried. Thinking back, he never brought anyone around me. My parents had something special. Part of him died with her and it seemed to be happening again. I didn't want to lose my father. I hoped he would recover and enjoy more life.

"Kasey, are you sure you're okay?" I asked for good measure.

"Baby, I'm fine. Eat something."

"I'm not so hungry."

We stayed at the hospital for most of the day. Nana went home to cook dinner. It was Sunday and I felt like I spoke to God all day. Kasey came back from Nana's with food for me. She said she was going home and I decided to go with her despite my fear that something would happen to dad while I was gone. I don't know what came over me. Watching my future wife undress made my dick rise to full attention. I came up behind her and palmed her full breasts massaging them gently. I turned her around sucking her nipples. I slowly backed her up to the bed, slowly laid her down. I opened her legs and teased her clit with my tongue and finally sucked it hard and made her orgasm. She couldn't take too much. She got on all fours and invited me to slide in. I didn't want to go crazy but damn, her pussy was so good. I stroked slow. Could not contain myself. I came so hard I was out of breath.

"Baby are you okay?" Kasey said.

"Yeah." I replied with ragged breath.

"You're worried about your dad. I understand."

"What if I lose him? He is the only parent I have left. I want him to meet the babies. I have been thinking all of these thoughts Sweets and they won't stop. Like he is supposed to guide me even now.

"We have to be positive."

"Please make up with your mother. I know that she's hard to deal with but, this situation with my dad... It makes me see what's really important."

"I am not sure I am ready to do that."

"Sweets, you only get one mother. We don't get to pick and choose. I now see that her antics, albeit a strange way to show it are about how much she loves you.

"I hear all that you are saying. I just feel like I am always being the bigger person. She is the mother."

We slept pretty well. Well I did, Kasey tossed & turned. She found it harder and harder to get comfortable these days. As the days went by, my dad was beginning to recover. First, he was learning exercises to help him begin exercising. These would gradually increase with his new rehabilitation program. Dad was also doing better with his diet. It was a slow transition that would last about six to twelve weeks. I was thankful that he was taking things seriously. He eventually began seeing a nutritionist and working with a personal trainer. I went to work out with him on occasion and witnessed him getting stronger. Things seemed to be in a better place for us as a family. Or so I thought.

Kasey

We were getting closer to my due date and I was getting bigger and bigger. The time had come for my baby shower. I'm glad it wasn't a surprise. I wanted to pick out something nice to wear and make sure my hair that had grown so much was done.

"Sweets, your makeup is flawless. Please come on. I promised your girls that I would have you there in a timely fashion."

"Yeah. Yeah. I'm coming."

"You look beautiful. You are radiant and glowing."

"Just remember that when I'm looking crazy because I'm taking care of your children." We pulled up to this nondescript location. It almost reminded me of a warehouse. It was huge with a parking lot full of cars. We walked into The Cat in The Hat themed baby shower. I love Dr. Seuss and my girls obviously know me very well. The colors were Red, White and Blue. Red and Blue Table cloths adorned the tables with white runners. There were red and white hats as centerpieces and fish bowls with gold fish on alternating tables. There was a beautiful three tier cake with the cat on it reading a book and the fish jumping out of the bowl. A candy table with red, white and blue gumballs, Swedish fish, twizzlers, cherry starbursts, shoelaces, blue gummy rings and rock candy lollipops. There was an entire table with coloring pages and crayons for the kids. My favorite thing, my nephews wearing thing 1 and thing 2 tee shirts. It was more than I expected.

Justin leaned in and whispered to me, "Nana made you a special cake for later."

"She did. Is it my favorite, the coconut with pineapple filling?"

"Of Course." I walked right over to her and kissed her cheek.

"I love you so much, Nana. Thanks for my special cake."

"Baby, it is the least I could do. Go say hello to the rest of your guests. We will talk later." There were so many people there. Even my supervisor, Judy and two coworkers, Dawn and Carlyne had come. Then my mother. I still had not done what Justin asked of me and called her to make amends. I guess I am stubborn like her. Why should I be the bigger person? She is my mother. She is supposed to love me unconditionally.

"Well daughter you look beautiful." Not at all what I expected.

"Thank you." Where was this conversation going? I was almost worried another argument would ensue at my shower.

"I want you to know I love you and I'm very proud of you. I'd like to spend the day with you soon. Before the babies come."

"Sure. Let's talk more later. I want to say hello to everyone." Clarke walked over and I'm assuming it was because my mom was talking to me.

"What was that about?" Clarke asked.

"She wants to hang out."

"That's different. It sounds like she's trying."

Krissy comes over to join the conversation.

I said to Krissy and Clarke. "Thanks so much, the shower, it's amazing."

"You need to thank your fiancé. He did most of the work." Clarke says.

"What? How? When?"

Krissy said, "Girl, he gave directions and we just assisted." I could not believe my future husband really listens to me.

"Don't start crying." Clarke says in a way that made us crack up.

As the shower wore on, it finally ended with me giving a speech thanking everyone that had attended.

"I would like to thank my almost-husband and friends for putting in the thought and taking the time to make this day special. I am thankful that Justin and I have so many people that care for us to share in the birth and lives of our children." We had so much stuff that my parents took some things to their house since we were moving soon. We were closer to closing on our new home, probably another month or two. I was dreading the move. I hate packing. Not that anyone likes packing, but I always start packing at the last minute when I travel because I hate it that much. My due date was a month and a half away. I wasn't sure I was going to make it. My last appointment, the doctor said if I made it another two weeks, he'd be happy with that. We didn't know what we were having.

Justin

The baby shower was great. I was sad that my dad was unable to make it to the shower. We promised we would visit with him. Every moment with him was a gift. Kasey and I had so much to celebrate and I felt grateful.

At 7am my phone woke me up vibrating against the nightstand next to me. I was exhausted and didn't want to move to even reach for it. Hoping it would soon stop, I felt Kasey nudging me to answer the call. I was thinking the worst as I reached out feeling for the phone and groggily answered, "Hello." I never fixed my eyes to see who was calling. All I could here was a crying woman. "Hello." I look at the phone to see it was Kelly. I sat up in the bed. Louder into the receiver, "Hello. Kelly?"

"It's me." Her sobs grew loudly in my ear, which gave me more angst.

"Kelly please calm down so I can understand you. I was thinking she was calling to tell me my father had passed. This was my worse fear. What's the matter? Is it my dad?"

"She's gone."

"Who is she? What are you saying?"

"Nana. Nana. She's gone!"

"Kelly hang up, I will be at the house in a few." I felt like I couldn't breathe. My heart was racing and hurting. I was dazed and confused, like the heavy weight champion of the world just uppercut me. Kasey was calling my name but, I didn't hear. She was in tears, standing in front of me, now yelling my name.

"Baby please tell me what's going on." I saw her lips moving and understood. I just couldn't respond. I was heartbroken. My grandmother had passed away. As I walked toward the bathroom, I could hear and feel Kasey behind me. I sat on the toilet seat as she stood in front of me. I finally found my voice and the words to explain the reality that had become my life. This changed the world as I knew it. She looked so sad as she waited for me to respond to her question. I know that she loved Nana as if she was her own grandmother.

As I approached Nana's apartment with trepidation, there were no smells wafting out the door of her apartment, no loud conversation or music being played. I knocked and my dad opened the door. I asked how he was and he just hugged me tightly. Uncle Joe and Kelly were in the living room. I asked Kelly, "Where is Bryan?"

"I asked Stephanie from down the hall if he could stay there until Nana…" She didn't even finish her sentence and began to cry all over again. Her eyes red and puffy from wiping fallen tears. The heaviness in the room, you could feel the void that had been created.

My uncle Joe explained that he had come by the house early to help my grandmother with some things around the house before church. He used his keys and called out to her. She did not respond. He went to the bedroom, she wasn't moving, he checked for a pulse and called 911. She was already gone. We watched as they carried her out and got on the elevator. I knew the days to come were going to be hard as we had lost the matriarch of our family.

The days following were quite somber. My emotions were quite mixed. On one hand, I was excited about the birth of my children. I was sad because I missed my grandmother. Kasey was growing increasingly uncomfortable from the pregnancy and often tossed and turned. It was the middle of the night and she was up again. "Babes, you okay." I asked.

"One of your children is relaxed on my bladder."

"Did you try to massage them over?"

"Yeah, but to where? Not much space in there." I had begun to rub her feet, just because.

"Thank you honey. Can't sleep again?" I had not been sleeping either in the past few weeks. It had been a tailspin. I had been having racing thoughts and night sweats a few times.

"No. At least there weren't any nightmares this time." I had been having a dream that I am running in Nana's hallway and she is standing in her doorway and I can smell food but, as

I get closer to her, the further she moves away. Several people suggested I talk to someone about my grief and loss. I needed to come down from it all first.

Kasey

We buried Nana, closed on our new home, moved all in three weeks. At this point, I was ready to deliver my babies. Dr. Z said we could deliver naturally provided no complications. My mother made good on our conversation at the shower. She had picked me up to go out for brunch.

"How do you like being back in the burbs?" Mom said.

"I honestly like the quiet more than I thought I would."

"I'd like to apologize to you for my behavior." I really thought I was in an alternate universe. Did she just apologize? I tell you this woman is crazy.

"I am very proud of the woman you have become."

"Thank you, but, if you're so proud then why do you ride me all the time as if I haven't gotten anything right?"

"Part of me sees that fighting spirit that I had as a girl. I am your mother and I have had hopes and dreams for you since you were in my womb. I am sure you are beginning to understand. Just promise me you will allow them to live the life they want and not what you envision." I wanted to fall out of my chair. They say becoming a grandparent is one of the greatest joys. Indeed, it is.

"Sus Abuelos, wanted to squelch the spirit. I wanted you to stand on your own two feet. Make sure you had a career that would ensure you did not have to depend on a man."

"Mom, I think I accomplished that."

"You have. I just hoped you'd be at a top law firm. After the education we paid for, I wasn't exactly happy with your choice of employment. I see that you are so much like me and you made your own decision despite how I felt."

"I learned all of those things from you."

"I'd like to help you with unpacking and decorating your new home, if that's okay?"

"Mom, I'd love that." I was happy to be starting this new relationship with my mother. It felt like there was so much to discover about this woman I called mother. I hoped that in time, I'd be able to call her friend. We ate while talking about paint colors and accents. When I got home, I went and got in bed immediately.

I must have slept for hours. It was difficult, so when it happened, I didn't fight it. My almost husband arrived with Thai food from Spice! I was all too happy because I was in no mood to cook. Unpacking the delectable dishes and sitting them on the breakfast bar.

Justin asks me, "How was brunch with your mom?"

"Amazing!" I reached in the cabinet to get a set of plates and opened the draw for utensils and placed them on the breakfast bar with the food. My hunger was so great, I could have skipped the plates and just used the fork to eat out of the container. I looked at Justin about to ask if he wanted the usual and he gave me a look like, are you okay?
I smirked rolling my eyes. "Don't give me that look. I am hoping that our relationship will change for the better."

"I am happy to hear that."

***

Monday came and I had my doctor's appointment.

Dr. Z our OB said, "I know you are uncomfortable. Everything looks good. Both babies are facing down. Looks like we can do it vaginally."

"That is good." I was relived because I didn't want to have a c-section which I felt would leave me in a lot of pain. Everything was going according to plan so when I left the hospital, I walked around a bit. Feeling exhausted and hungry, I called Clarke to see if she could get out for lunch.

"Hey, can you do lunch?"

"Yeah, meet me at Patsy's on 69th and 1st."

When I arrived, it was fairly empty. The hostess sat me at a table for two and immediately the waitress brought me water.

"You looked like you may be thirsty."

"Thanks."

"Do you want to wait for the other person to order?"

I took a sip. "Yes, thank you."

"I'm Tammy and I will be your server." Tammy walked away and I pulled out my phone. I already knew I wanted a pizza. No sooner than I started checking emails, Clarke walks in. We greeted each other and she sat.

"You look ready."

"I'm beyond ready. These god children of yours are on notice."

"I can only imagine." We chatted and Clarke needed to run back to work. I took a stroll around the area and thought about how my life was about to change. *Who would the babies look like? How am I going to manage being a mother of two? What would life be like as a wife?* I just wanted to remember to communicate as best I could to Justin so we would be on the same page.

I got home and put my feet up. They had become swollen due to all the walking. I was constantly fatigued. According to Dr. Z, it was normal. Later that evening while lying in bed, I got a sharp back pain. Then it felt like cramping.

"Honey, I think I'm having contractions."

"Do we need to go to the hospital?"

"I don't think so. We should monitor them. That way when they are close together, we know to go down." I tossed and turned, while he slept like a baby. I dozed here and there but, not a deep sleep. I went and sat in the comfy chair and ended up falling asleep. At about 3:30am, I woke up and stood up, another contraction. Then I noticed something trickling down my legs. My water broke. I made my way to the bathroom to clean up as quickly as I could. I thought that I would get dressed then wake Justin up. I made my way to our bed room to wake him when another strong contraction hit me. The contractions were about 7 minutes apart. I woke Justin up so we could go to the hospital.

"Jus, Jus, honey I need you to wake up."

"Is it time?" He jumped out of bed, threw on sweats and bolted toward the door. I stood at the door with the keys in one hand and bag in the other.

"I think you forgot some things." Handed him the keys and his wallet and he picked up the bag. As he drove, I attempted to breathe through the contractions. It took about 30 minutes to get to Manhattan. Another few minutes I would be having these babies in the back of their daddy's charger.

Justin

I tried not to panic but, I was a mess. I did not want to deliver the children and I didn't want them to be born in the car. When the contractions hit, she wanted silence. I put the easy jazz station on as requested. In about thirty minutes and no traffic, we made it to the hospital.

"Babe, I'm feeling wet again."

"I thought your water broke already."

"Me too." Up the elevator to 7th floor. When we got to Labor and Delivery a young lady from our church was at the front desk working.

"Hey Tasha, we didn't know you did this shift." I said.

"Overtime." The triage nurse came over and asked a series of questions. Tasha was kind enough to complete our paperwork, while we went to get checked. She was about five centimeters dilated. They said the contractions are progressing like they should. They checked the babies heart beats and both were strong. You hear about stories where people get sent home, but she had progressed so far and due to having twins we stayed.

Her parents arrived about fifteen minutes after we got settled. I called my dad and he said to call him when they came and he would be on the way.

"Babe please get me ice chips. My mouth feels dry." I read the first time a woman gives birth can take time. I was ready to be there forever waiting to meet them. Her contractions were back to back. "I feel like I need to push."

"That's my cue to go to the waiting room." Her dad said.

I guess having twins was speeding up the process because it had only been three hours since we arrived at the hospital. I thought it would take longer. They were six weeks early but, right on time. I was silently praying that they would be well. Another contraction came as Dr. Z came in to deliver the babies. He and the nurses, Katie and Lisa were setting things up.

"Okay Kasey, I need a big push. I can see baby A's head."

"Come on baby you can do this." I said.

"Push!" Lisa said. She then counted 1-2-3-4-5-6-7-8-9-10

Katie jumped in, “Take a deep breath for me Kasey”

They both counted again.

Another deep breath.

Dr. Z said, “Push Kasey with all you’ve got!”

Baby A, a little boy, our baby boy was born. Her mother went with him to be checked out.

"Kasey, how are you feeling?”, I asked.

"Tired, but like I need to push again."

"Seems like they were right on top of one another. When you get the next contraction, you're going to give me another big push." Dr. Z said in his burly voice. That contraction came and my future wife pushed half the baby out. Dr. Z told her to wait as he cleaned baby B’s mouth. The cord also seemed to be a little tangled around the baby’s neck, so he removed that as well.

Dr. Z made me a little nervous because he did not say anything at first but, then
“Kasey, on the next contraction, push.” The next contraction came, she bared down and pushed and baby B, my little princess was born. Then I cried. It was so beautiful. I witnessed the most wonderful thing. I went to get her dad and call mine. They cried with me. I was very proud of her mother who was a great help. I had so much respect for the woman I was going to marry.

Kasey

It was hard but, I did it. I can't even describe all the emotions I was feeling. I love my Jacob and Jade. They are precious and I thanked God for safe passage from my womb to earth. They are two great reasons to lose sleep. As the days went on, there were lots of visitors. Family, friends and gifts were still pouring in from people we knew and didn't know. Those we didn't know were friends of Nana. I missed her love, spirit and kindness. I knew she would have wanted me to be filled with joy. I could feel her presence all around us. There were times the babies would be staring off into space but, smiling. I imagined Nana was there smiling back at them.

When night fell and it was just the four of us, I thought about the things I wanted for my life. I looked at the babies while they slept and felt full. My cup was overflowing. Jade liked to snuggle. Jacob was super squirmy. Skin to skin for both babies was calming. Justin would have one while I had the other. It was how our family bonded.

One night after putting the babies down for bed, I said to him, "Babe."

"Yeah Sweets."

"Let's write a list of what we want in life moving forward."

"Top of the list. Our wedding!"

"Agreed."

“I would like to keep it simple.”

“Sweets, you, simple? Those two words don’t go in the same sentence with you?”

“Very funny. I just want the ceremony to be intimate. Maybe a modest reception.”

“You’re serious.”

“Yes. I am. I want to spend wisely. We have two others to think of moving forward.”

“We do.”

We both looked at the babies and smiled. They were swaddled and sleeping comfortably.

“Can you believe we did this?” Justin asked.

“Sometimes yes and sometimes no.”

“I am glad we had no complications. Thankful that Dad is here to spend time with them as they grow. Grateful that you and your mother are on better terms and still missing Nana so much it hurts.”

“I was thinking about her too. She would be so elated. I know her spirit is with us.”

I went to sleep after we finished our list and talking with visions of what my wedding day would look like and smiling because despite the challenges, life was good.

Part 2

Camille & Hunter

God, a Minister & Us

Camille

We have resolved to hellos and goodbyes whenever we entered and left each other's presence. Sleeping together or not and being cordial had become our norm, but it was not always this way. Being married to him used to be the greatest honor and now it was this awkward dance between myself and someone I was not sure I knew. Had we changed that much in the last five years? I'm not sure. Once upon a time, my husband, Hunter, was not only my significant other, but my friend, the person I told everything to. We used to have fun. The possibilities were endless on the adventures we would take.

We met through my friend, Liza who wasn't just my friend; she was more like the sister I never had. We met my sophomore year in college. She was a year ahead of me and it has been a blessing to have her in my life. Around Christmas, Liza swore that she had the perfect person for me to meet. I resisted for six months because I had no desire to meet anyone. I'd met and dated the most awful men, in a variety of places... church, lounges, work, clubs and the list continued. The worst dating experience was with the bus driver. I thought he would be a decent guy. He was obviously employed; he was nice looking and he took an interesting approach to get my phone number. One Sunday morning on my way to church, I got on the bus and being polite, I greeted the driver, "Good morning." then head to the back of the bus as I always do. As we neared my stop, I pulled the cord to signal stop requested. Holding on the poles as I navigated down the few steps to the back door. When I went to press the yellow tape for the door to open, I realized the green light wasn't lit. As any New Yorker would do, I yelled, "Back Door." I looked toward the front to see him in the mirror waving me to come to the front of the bus.

I get to the front of the bus, which was a few short paces. "You didn't hear me yell, back door? You are going to make me late to church."

"Yeah, but I wanted to get your number."

"You waited until now for that?" I chuckled at him.

"What's your name?"

"Camille. Yours?"

"Travis. You going to give me your number so I can call you?"

"You can give me your number and maybe I will call you."

Shaking his head at me with a grin he said, "Okay, I see you." I pulled out my phone and added his name and number into my contacts. "Am I free to go now?"

"Absolutely, just make sure I hear from you." And just like that, the front doors opened and I was free to go. I smiled and shook my head all the up the block to church. I couldn't believe he would make me and the few other riders late because he wanted my name and number. I was super flattered and thought it was a creative way to gain my attention.

About two days went by and I sent him a text. *Hey it's Camille. I met you on the M2 bus. Wanted to see when you were free to hang out.* It was a few hours before I got a response, but it wasn't via text. My phone started to ring and the name on the screen read Travis, MTA.

"Hey, it's Travis, what's up?"

"Nothing much."

"Hold on a sec." He obviously had another call. It was short lived. "Hello. You free tomorrow?"

"I could be. What's up?" I didn't want to sound too eager.

"I was thinking we could have drinks."

"Cool. Where do you want to meet me?"

To my surprise he said, "Meet you, no, I will pick you up."

"Okay, I will text the address."

"Noted. I'm looking forward to spending time with you Camille."

I was cheesing. "That's sweet. See you tomorrow."

"See you and don't forget to text the address."

Travis picked me up in his what appeared to be a freshly washed 1969 Camaro painted black. He got out the car and opened the door for me. When he got in the car, we began talking about nothing in particular. He was presenting to be a genuine gentleman. He parked his car in a garage for the night. I was glad it wasn't far. I had on my cute heels, jeans and a crop top. We ended up at a comedy show. I am not usually into comedy, but I must admit it was funny. The drinks were good and perfectly mixed. I also ordered some appetizers, just to coat my stomach. Things were going well until we started discussing personal information.

"Do you have children?" He asked. Of course, I am wondering where this line of questioning is going.

"No, I don't. Do you?"

"Yes, I have three." I was immediately turned off. I generally didn't date men with children, let alone three children.

"How often do you get to see them?"

"Every weekend, but I have to go and pick them all up from their mothers' houses."

"Did you say, houses? As in multiple mothers?"

"Yeah they all have different mothers." He took another sip of his drink like having three baby mothers wasn't an issue.

"Oh." My face obviously did not mask my horror to this revelation. The date went south from there. I could not believe this man had three children by three different women and was so casual about it. He also had the audacity to call me selfish because I said I didn't date men with children. I was baffled at his attitude. It is a preference, not a judgement.

He shifted in his chair. "I wouldn't have thought that a woman like you would judge me because of my past."

"I'm not judging you. I was just taken aback. I just wasn't expecting to hear that your children had multiple mothers."

"I don't have kids everywhere? I have three kids that I take care of and I'm active in their lives."

"Great for you, but that is a bit much for me." I know me and my facial expressions were probably adding insult to injury.

"Are you kidding me right now?" His nostrils flared while his chest dropped deeply in with each breath.

"Look, I just believe in a family unit. You know, being together under one roof." I gulped the last of my drink. The show had been over for about fifteen minutes and he waved down the waitress and asked for the check.

"Women like you make it hard for men like me." He retrieved his wallet from his back pocket paid the bill. "And for the record, I was 16-years old when I had my first, 24-years old when I had my second and 29-years old when I had my last. I wasn't out here making babies with any and every girl I met. I was in relationships with my children's mothers." He was proud, maybe not about having three children by three different women, but proud that he was actively parenting all three. I found that admirable, but not something that I was willing to take on.

Before I could say anything further, we were leaving the lounge. He was a genuinely nice guy because even after that uncomfortable interaction he walked me home. Travis and I never spoke again and after several bad dates that included this guy, John who had stalker tendencies, Anthony who brought his ex-girlfriend on the date and at this juncture, I was in a place where I had no desire to meet Liza's fix up.

In the wake of summer, Fourth of July weekend, Liza had a barbecue. Liza and her husband, Josh have lived in their new home for about a year. It was a beautiful wrap around porch with a deck off the kitchen. My favorite part is the swing on the front porch. We spent lots of time on the swing talking and enjoy each other's company. Little did I know, I'd meet my husband that day.

When I arrived, it was only a few people there, most I knew. Hunter was having a beer and I noticed him but, tried not to give his 6'4", muscular, full lips, bald head, nice full beard, tight butt, well dressed, butter pecan skinned self too much attention. He was gorgeous! Liza came out of the kitchen onto the patio carrying a salad and caught me gawking.

"Cam!" She snickered as she passed by me and sat the bowl on the table.
I was totally caught off guard, "Yeah."

As she walked back toward the sliding door. "Come with me to get some more stuff from the kitchen." I already knew how this conversation was going to go. If I was interested in someone, Liza always had a mouthful to say.

"You need a napkin to get that drool off your chin?" She and I laughed.

"No! Was I staring that hard?"

"Cam, if you stared any harder you would have been able to tell what label underwear the man had on." I was intrigued to say the least. "Who is that guy?"

"Only the man I've been trying to set you up with."

"That can't be Hunter." I couldn't believe what I saw. I mean, I was a tad shocked.

"Yes, it is."

"Introduce us."

"Hmmm, let me think... ummm, no!"

"Cold Liza, real cold." Liza obviously wanted me to sweat a bit before the introductions because I waited so long to agree. Hunter appeared to be engaged in the man talk that was taking place. I went to pour some sangria in my cup and make a small plate. As I walked to the table with the food, I tried so hard not to glance. When I did, we made eye contact. I felt the blood from my body rush to the center of me. The pulsating rhythm now taking place reminding me how long it had been since I had been touched, licked and kissed. I could only imagine what magical things our bodies could do once they met.

About an hour later, it looked like Hunter was about to leave. I had just come out of the house from the bathroom and saw him offering handshakes to the guys, giving Liza a kiss on the cheek and heading towards the patio door where I was.

"Thought you would never come back." I was surprised that he was waiting on me. He hadn't given me the time of day. He threw his beer bottle in the trash can and smiled. There was that blood rush again.

"I wasn't gone that long." I said while biting my lip so I wouldn't focus on the throbbing now happening between my legs. I could smell his cologne. Subtle yet, effective.

"I have to leave, but here is my card."

"I don't understand. All this time and you said nothing." I took his card and slipped it into my back pocket after giving it a once over.

"I came here to meet you, but Liza's entertaining and being a great hostess and I decided I would take matters into my own hands. She and Josh have mentioned you on multiple occasions. They wanted us to meet a while ago."

"Well, since you know all about me, I guess I should tell you that my name is Camille." I stuck my hand out to shake his.

"I know your name and I'm sure you know mine, but I'm Hunter. Give me a call." He had taken my hand into his and gently squeezed. His hands were soft like he used shea butter daily.

"I definitely will." Looking into his eyes, I was excited about the possibilities and knew it wouldn't be long before I gave him a call. Just as quickly as he came to me, he quickly left. I was seriously stuck for a minute. The rest of the barbecue was uneventful for me because I was focused on the man who introduced himself and dashed out.

When I called on a Wednesday afternoon, my stomach was in knots. I am okay with calling guys and making the first move but this, this was different. It was midday and I was outside having lunch when I scrolled through my contacts and pressed send. The phone rang twice, and upon answering, it sounded like lots of yelling in the background then finally his voice came through.

"Hello, this is Hunter."

"This is Camille.

“Hey. How are you?”

“I’m doing okay. It sounds like you’re in the middle of something. If you are busy, we can talk later."

"No, I'm good to talk for a bit. Nice to hear from you."

I could tell he left the area he was in because the noise dissipated. Then I had to gather all of my nerve. "It’s nice to hear from you, as well. I am not usually this forward, but would you like to get together for drinks this Friday?" I was nervous but, Rotten Apple girl to the core. I shook those nerves and bucked up.

"I would love to spend time with you, but I am going out of town Friday morning."

"Oh, okay.” I tried to hide my obvious disappointment, “I guess some other time then." I was deflated, put myself out there to be rejected. I was done. Dating is the most difficult thing ever. There is all this pressure to be your authentic self and then you meet these men with all these issues, baby mama drama, stalkers and those who just trying to have sex with everyone they meet.

"Camille don't give up so easy. If you aren't busy, tomorrow night is cool."

Well, that wasn’t expected. "Sure, where should we go?"

"There is a spot called MOCA, let’s say 6:30."

"I know that place.”

“Okay, great. Look, I have to go.” The background noise seemed to have returned.

"I'll see you tomorrow."

"See you then."

****

I was elated to have the opportunity to keep company with this man, find out what he was all about. I mean, he obviously was attractive but I know looks aren't everything. I arrived fifteen minutes early to MOCA as always, I was early to everything. My mother instilled that being late was rude unless totally unavoidable and beyond your control. I sat on the far side of the bar so we would be in one another's view when he walked in. It was twenty minutes later and ten minutes past when we were to meet. I was beginning to get anxious and aggravated. No one wants to be stood up. My phone buzzed just as I began to think of all the previous dates that were not so great. I read the text message; *I'm looking for a park.* Okay, so he did not stand me up and was not miserably late. At least he had the courtesy to send a message that he was in the area. When he walked into the lounge, I had to take a sip of my drink, looking at this specimen of a man was making excited. Hunter had SWAG. He was casually dressed, but it was just how he moved that gave him an extra quality of sex appeal, it was effortless movement. I watched as he scanned the room then, our eyes met and he walked the short distance. Before taking a seat on the stool next to me he gently kissed my cheek. His cologne was intoxicating. The butterflies in my belly danced as they moved south. I took another sip to calm myself.

"Nice to see you, again." I was silently saying, *Dear God, please let him be "the one",.*

"You too."

"Have you been waiting long?"

"No, not really. Just long enough for me to respond to a few emails." He got the bartender's attention to order a drink for himself.

"May I have Jameson?" He said to the bartender. "Would you like another?" I was pretty much finished what I had been sipping on.

"Yes. Please." I responded to him. "Can I have another rough sex?" I said to the bartender.

"No problem. Would you like some time to look at the menu?"

"Thanks." He said. "Rough Sex." He smirked.

"It's the name of the drink." I laughed.

We engaged in a bit of small talk, then I asked, "So, what do you do?"

"Getting straight to the point, huh?" He smiled and I gave him a nod.

"I thought it was small talk." I laughed.

"I'm an Iron Worker, We Build This City." He said that as if he was advertising for his job.

"You build buildings?"

"No, I actually put the beams up before the building is built."

"Sounds high up." The thought of being that high up made my stomach do a small flip. He chooses to be up there every day.

"Yeah it is." He then showed me a video he recorded while at work.

"OMG. That is crazy. Tell me the scariest thing that has happened up there."

He stopped for a minute to think about it and took another sip of his drink. "Well, we were 80 feet in the air working on the roof of a building. A torrential rain had begun to come down about 11:30ish. There was no rain in the forecast. The sun was quickly covered by clouds and the sky got black. While on the beam, I wasn't completely tied off and slipped. I grabbed hold of the closest column until my boys came and got me. We slowly moved to safety.

"Oh wow! That's crazy. I would have freaked out. I am not thrilled about heights."

"I love what I do. If I didn't, a situation like that would have made me quit. I like building things. Seeing something go from nothing but beams to beautiful completed architecture." This was a different kind of turn on. A man who is passionate about the work he does.

Hunter had finished two years of college but after that, didn't know what he wanted to do. His cousin, Knowledge, put him on to iron work. Apparently, Knowledge also put him on to the blatant racist humor.

"Every conversation that I have has to be calculated with persons that are not of color. One day a cop car was passing by, someone made a comment, 'Hey, who did you rob today? They are coming to get you.' These are just some of the few inappropriate comments that are made. You have to laugh them off and worse things have happened. I have made myself more palatable and it has paid off, but that doesn't make it any easier."

"Do you think that you are putting on a show sometimes?"

"You know, sometimes I wonder if I am pouring it on thick, but I realize that I am a black man and although my work speaks for itself, it isn't enough." Hearing these things made me cringe. I know racism still happens, but damn. To deal with that daily because people have preconceived notions about who you are and what you are about because you are black. Hunter had just completed the three-year training to become an official Iron Worker.

"While in training we are called Journeymen. It's a lot of grunt work. Taking orders for the seasoned guys, hazing if you will. Hunter was born and raised in Brooklyn and he still lives there. His mother allows him to stay in the basement apartment, which he pays rent for. She informed him after graduating from high school that laying around her home was not an option. Everything about her sounded strong. She was educated, worked all while ensuring her children got the best education possible. Not only that, they were exposed to the arts. New Yorkers often stay in their boroughs and aren't able to experience all the city has to offer but, Ms. Douglas ensured that her children would see more than just Brooklyn.

"My mother used to say that she wanted us to be happy and productive members of society. She didn't raise no junk. We had work or go to school. Laying around wasn't an option in her home." She sounded like the mother I want to be one day.

Hunter

Once upon a time my wife was so easy going. We had fun all the time, we called them our adventures. Her spirit was free. Now she is pensive and the air between us always tense. I would love to go back to the endless conversations and our easygoing interactions. I remember our first date on an early warm summer night I left feeling like I just found what I had been looking for. At 27, I was ready to go back to school to get my Bachelor's degree in business to start my own company. I was making a nice living with my career as an iron worker. I had been doing iron work for three years and realized I had a knack for building, so I saved by staying in my mom's basement apartment. I was thriving in every area of my life. But something was missing that I couldn't fill with just anything or anyone. That thing missing was a woman to share life with.

When I walked into the bar, I didn't immediately see her. I looked around and our eyes met. Her bronzed skin, light make up, long dress was perfect. Even sitting, her body was perfect. I loved every curve as I casually took in the view. I walked over. When I sat down next to her, I could smell her sweet scent. I ordered a Jameson on the rocks.

"What exactly is it that you do? Liza mentioned working with kids."

"I'm in school full time and run an after-school program and day camp."

"What are you in school for?"

"My masters in special education and social work."

"Dual degree. Nice."

"I want it to be over already. Going through the summer will allow me to finish next spring." Damn, she was beautiful and educated. Together we could be a power couple.

"What do you do for fun?"

"I like swimming and white-water rafting. Of course, only in the summer months. I am a movie buff as well."

"Rafting? I'm impressed. Have you done rock climbing or skydiving?"

"Skydiving? I'm not that bold and indoor rock climbing only once."

"Well maybe you will embrace your bold side and we can skydive together."

She gave me a look and replied. "Ummm, let me think about that." We laughed.
Camille said she was the youngest of four children and the only girl.

"My parents are protective, let me get my way sometimes, but I am definitely no stranger to the word no. My oldest brother and I aren't super close, he was on his way out of the house a few years after I was born. My other two brothers, are also protective and made sure I was good."

"Oh so, everyone does what you say?"

"I wouldn't say that?"

"Sounds like you are spoiled." She swatted my hand. Her hands were so soft, nicely manicure, natural polish, no tips, just her.

"Maybe a little if I am being honest." We laughed knowing that it probably wasn't a little.

"It doesn't bother me; I am the oldest of three myself."

We ordered some food and kind of lost track of time. She pulled her phone out of her purse and checked the time.

"I guess I better get out of here. I have a very busy day tomorrow."

"What time is it?"

"12:10am." I pulled out my phone from my hip.

"Wow. That went faster than I thought. I think I'd like to spend more time with you."

"Do you now?" She said with a grin. I could see she was not trying to give her entire hand away. This evening left me planning our next encounter. I was hoping she would be down.

***

While I was away, I called Camille. I wanted my intentions to be clear. We spoke for about an hour.

"Why are you in ATL?" I heard her television on in the background.

"Has anyone ever told you that you ask a lot of questions?"

"Yes, my 1st grade teacher, Ms. Oliver. How do you get information if you don't ask questions?"

"I see." I paused because I wasn't sure I wanted to discuss my parents' marriage. "I am visiting my dad."

"Does he live there? I assumed your parents were together in Brooklyn."

"No, they are divorced."

"Sorry to hear that."

"They get along great. Sometimes too good. They are the couple that should never live together."

"Wow, maybe they will one day get back together."

"Now, I see."

"See what?"

"You are the eternal optimist."

"I guess." I didn't know if I made her uncomfortable. So, I changed the subject.

"Are you having a Netflix and chill with your bonnet on and a glass of wine?"

"Comedy must be your new profession. The television is on, but nothing in particular."

"Mmmhuh, but you not denying the bonnet? We started laughing.

"You are so silly."

"I aim to please." We laughed often. It was the best part of being together. We could have serious conversations, but we always found room to laugh.

By the end of our call, I learned that her parents lived in Brewster, NY about an hour north from the City and that her brothers lived in different cities around the country.

Camille

I used to think he would always have me, catch me when I fell, but I was wrong. On our second date, we met at Brooklyn Boulders. Arriving at the same time, we greeted each other with kisses on the cheeks and headed inside. Every touch, every kiss, every embrace my body responded, with butterflies in my stomach and created a pulsating clitoris. I squeezed my thighs together.

After checking in and getting our equipment we met our instructor. We changed shoes and met Jake by the wall. He taught us fundamental climbing techniques, risk management, how to tie off knots, fit into the harness correctly and belaying, which means to use the equipment to manage the rope of your climbing partner. Jake asked which of us wanted to go first. Hunter volunteered me to go first.

"Me, go first?"

"Yeah, why not?" I gave a hard eye roll and he laughed.

Jake said, "Remember, to use your terms. On Belay and Belaying on to communicate with one another.".

I said, "On Belay."

Hunter responded, "Belaying on." I slowly began to climb up the wall. Not realizing that I had gone pretty high up. I took a minute to pause. When I looked down, I realized the floor was far away. My stomach got butterflies, but not the good ones. I was scared. It is that feeling when you are on a roller coaster and you go on a drop.

"Are you okay up there?" I heard Hunter call out. I guess he too realized I had paused movement for a few moments.

"I think I'm ready to come down." I was starting to feel a little nauseous.

"Are you sure you don't want to keep going, you are halfway to the top? I got you!" That was reassuring.

Not wanting to punk out. I took a deep breath and kept it moving. And, I made it to the top. I yelled. "I did it!"

"Yeah you did, ready to descend."

"Yes." I was proud of myself for going to the top.

When I got to the ground, Hunter said, "You did good." He smiled at me and gave me a tight hug. I could have lived in that for days. It was warm, securing, comforting and I felt at peace. It helped that he smelled so good.

Hunter

The coaching session was just an hour. Camille only went all the way up once. I think she was done after that. I was excited that she tried something she'd only done once. It was definitely a date to remember. We met at the front after coming out of the locker room. I didn't really work up a sweat, but still wanted to wipe and swipe some extra deodorant on.

"What are you hungry for?" I asked her as we walked to the car.

"Nothing in particular." She said. I loved that Camille was rather easygoing.

"Feel like dancing?"

"In these clothes?" She shrieked. "It is a weeknight. Shouldn't we plan that for a weekend?"

"You are assuming there will be a date three."

"WOW, maybe not." Her face full of shock.

"Just messing with you." At least she has a tough skin and didn't get all sensitive.

"Do you eat Mexican?"

"Yes."

"Okay, let's go to Lobo." We got in my car and talked on the way. It seemed as if we never ran out of things to say then. It was a beautiful evening. I rolled down the windows slightly letting the breeze wash over us as we chatted.

“That was really fun. I think that was the most creative date I have ever experienced.”

“I’m glad you enjoyed yourself. Be honest you were freaking out when you were half way up?” I chuckled thinking about her face while she was on the climbing wall.

“Are you laughing?”

“Yes, I am sorry but your face up there was priceless.”

“I was scared but, I did it.”

“Yes, and that is what counts.”

We arrived to Lobo, sat down at our table and continued our conversation after ordering drinks. Then it happened, she asked **That Question**.

“Why are you single?"

"I have high standards. I like a woman that can and will do for herself, but can appreciate a man taking care of her, too. I could ask you the same."

"I hear you. Well guys I have met are messy."

"Messy?"

"Yes, messy. Several children, baby momma drama, no job, no skills, I just got out of jail, I live with my momma, smoke weed and freeload, I just want to have sex and my all-time favorite... I'm married. I've heard it all, so I took a break from dating. I thought I would get to know me better."

"Dating is difficult. I have run into similar things. The worst was this chick I met that wanted me to be her personal ATM. Date three and she was attempting to get me to give up money for her hair and nails. I was like... Amazed at the audacity and nerve of her. I'm still in shock. She actually attempted to friend me recently... Blocked her!"

"Ha. I can do you one better. I meet this guy. He seemed cool. We planned to go out to dinner. He picks me up. Late. I did not trip, but he showed up with someone in the front seat. I think okay, maybe he has to drop her off somewhere. When I get in, he introduces her as Stacey. I am like, nice to meet you, until I realize she is the mother of his child." My face must have had the look of shock and confusion on it.

"He brought the baby momma on a date? WOW!"

"Yes, he did. When we pulled up to the lounge, she got out with us and I was in shock and dismay. Needless to say, he and I never went out again. She was cool."

"You are better than I am. Why would she even want to be out with him on a date? Strange."

I loved talking to Camille. She was honest, fun and easygoing. After drinks, eating big burritos and guacamole, I drove her home to Harlem. I was interested in continuing the conversation and I wasn't about to make her take the train.

Camille

I was impressed he dropped me home. After all the bad dates I have had, you just never know what will happen. It wasn't early, but not late, you know

MTA is never going your way. I was glad I didn't have to contend with the 2 and 3 trains. Hunter surprised me and I appreciated that he was concerned about my welfare. Refusing to have me take the train. He opened my door and I got out. We gave a warm hug and he lightly kissed me on my lips.

"See you soon."

"Absolutely."

As I entered the elevator, I was thinking that Hunter kind of feels too good to be true. My cell was ringing and broke my silent thoughts.

"Hey Liza." I said, putting my bag down. "Well, how was it?"

"He was a gentleman. We had fun climbing and then had dinner at this Tex-Mex place, Lobo."

"I told you."

"I know, I know. We are going to Negril on Friday. He wants to dance."

"Sounds like you two are getting hot and heavy."

"Liza, I am not jumping or leaping into anything. Just going with the flow. I don't want to get my hopes up. Speaking of letting things flow, I better work on this paper otherwise I will be going nowhere."

"Talk to you later. Love you."

"Love you too sis."

After completing the frame of my paper and crawling into bed, I began thinking about what life would be like with Hunter. He was strong, a gentleman and I could see he had the ability to be vulnerable. That was apparent when he talked about his parents' marriage. I began exploring my body with my fingers while I stared at the ceiling. Making my nipples hard. Feeling the wetness coming from my vagina. The fire between my legs needed to be put out. After thinking of Hunter's strong hug, the smell of his skin, those full lips that lightly touched mine, I wanted to taste his tongue from a more intimate kiss that was yet to be had. I reached for my familiar *helper, in the cigar box on my nightstand.* Twisting it from off to on, I only needed one speed and that was high. The hum of my *helper* was soothing. After teasing my clitoris and then finding the spot that would bring me to climax, I came so hard. Hunter had me open, I will admit, but that was my little secret.

When Hunter and I first began dating, I had so many dreams of what our lives would become, how we would grow individually and together. It was all so fascinating in the beginning. Our third date, we went to the West Village, there was dinner and dancing at Negril. As I was putting the finishing touches on my make up, I heard the intercom ring. "Hunter." I spoke into the box. "Yes." I was excited and had to take a deep breath. I stood at the door waiting for him to come down the hall from the elevator. He greeted me with a kiss on the cheek, holding a gorgeous bouquet. Hunter further impressed me by showing me his creativity. It was a mixture of birds of paradise, lilies, and cattleya orchids. Making an impression. I loved it.

"Why, thank you." Taking the bouquet, I invited him in. Once inside, I gave him the lightest kiss on the lips.

"I can see you weren't expecting this."

"No, I wasn't. They are beautiful."

"Ready?"

"Yes, let me put these in water, grab some flats and we can go."

We had dinner upstairs at Negril which was designed for dining only. Their rum punch was good, really good and I enjoyed it just a bit too much. I was feeling nice. I had a glass of water after returning from the bathroom. When I stood up it was obvious, I was feeling the impact of the rum punch. I had to steady myself before walking away from the table to use the restroom. Once the bill had been paid, we went downstairs to where the lounge of Negril was and people were sitting and drinking but, not really dancing. We got more drinks and the beat of the music was feeling good to me. I started to two-step and he followed my lead. The music changed up and some reggae came on. We danced on top of one another, grinding. We closed the place down that night. On the way back to the car, he grabbed my hand. Maybe because he knew I was still slightly inebriated or he was trying to get close. Either way, I welcomed his touch. It had been a while since I was close to anyone. I got in the car and he closed the door behind me. He got in and started the car. He looked at me and I at him. We kissed. It was the most passionate kiss I had in my life. It was sensual, not sloppy. Gentle, not down the throat with tongue. My vagina had awakened, moistened and was pulsating. We broke our embrace and I took a deep breath. We just looked at each other. He broke the silence.

"Breakfast?"

"Sure." I said, as I opened the window. I needed to catch my breath after that kiss.

"IHOP?"

"Oh yes! I got this one."

Hunter

Camille was tipsy but, not sloppy drunk. The more time I spent with her, the more I like what I was seeing. A woman who is willing to share financial responsibility too, I mean it was just IHOP, but still she didn't expect me to pay for everything. We went to the 14th street location and ate like we missed a few meals. I ordered a T- Bone Steak and Eggs and she got a Bacon Temptation Omelette.

"You going to eat all of that?" I said as the waiter walked away from the table after taking our order.

"Maybe, maybe not, but I am going to try." We laughed.

"Dancing was fun. It is been a while since I have done that."

"Honestly, me too. Lots of my friends are married and have children. The others don't live in New York."

"I hear you. I am kind of in the same boat. Mostly tend to hang out with Knowledge and Josh after work at the bar."

"Why do they call him Knowledge?"

"Growing up on the block he was super smart and knew random stuff. He got along with everyone. He was respected by the smart kids and the thugs."

"Makes sense."

"Knowledge is only three years older than I, but he looked out for me like a brother."

By the time we were leaving, the sun was coming up. I drove her home and she kissed me goodbye, tasting of syrup. I went to get out to open her door.

"Stay, it's okay." She said.

"Talk to you later?"

"Yes." I kissed her again. My dick grew to a full erection. I watched that beautiful booty go inside the building and disappear on the elevator. I took off and I flew down the FDR. There were very few vehicles on the road. When I got home, I stripped and crashed.

When I woke which was about six hours later, my cell was buzzing.

"Where you been? I've been attempting to reach you." I honestly turned my phone off until we got in the car to take Camille home. I wanted to disconnect and just enjoy her company.

"Out."

"With who?"

“I'm older, stop asking me so many questions. What's up Drew?" My younger sister liked to keep tabs on me.

"Mom wanted you to come up and help her."

"Help her do what?"

"I don't know. Brother, seriously, where were you?"

"What's the matter? You seem worried."

"I just don't like when I call and you don't answer and I sent text messages that went unanswered." My sister is the youngest of my siblings. She's afraid I will leave like my dad. She thinks she is the boss of me. Her attachment to me is due to our parents’ divorce. She was young, when it all happened. Wayne, my brother behaved indifferent, but that was his personality overall. He didn’t have a flat affect but, just neutral. With my dad moving so far away, I stepped up at times. We all love him and he has made as much time for the three of us as possible being miles away. I don’t presume to understand why he went so far away, but I think he was hurt and retreated to what was comfortable. I went up to my mom's house and she was attempting to put together some shelves.

"Hey Momma."

"Hunter, you look happy, what's her name?"

"Whose name?"

"The young lady that has you looking goofy."

"Mom, I don't know what you mean."

"Hunter, I know you all too well. Hope this one stays around and I get to meet her." My mother does know me, but I wasn't ready to discuss my dates with Camille.

"Who are we meeting?" Drew jumped in.

"No one. How are the lessons going?" I said changing the subject.

"Good, want to hear?" She played a piece by Chopin. My sister was wicked on the piano and was able to play all sorts of genres. Juilliard was her goal. Drew also had great grades as well. When she was done. We clapped and she left the room. I helped my mom finish all the chores she could pack in two hours.

"Hunter, whenever you are ready, I'm here to hear about this new person in your life."

"Alright mom." I knew she waited until Drew was out of earshot to bring it up again.

Camille

In the early days, Hunter responded to my text almost immediately. We would go back and forth when we were not able to speak. Then when we could speak, we would talk for what felt like hours. That first summer of dating, we had done so many things. The best was the surprise whitewater rafting trip for my birthday. Somehow, he managed to coordinate with Liza to have a couple's trip. He refused to tell me where we were going. The ride was torture. When we finally got close the signs gave it away.

"Hunter are we going rafting?"

"Yes, Honeypot."

"Oh yes! This is an awesome birthday trip. Thank you." When we got there, we met up with Liza and Josh, his good friend, Justin and his girl, Kasey, my cousin Sheena and her flavor of the month and

Knowledge and his wife, Toni. It was cool that he could pull this off. All the ladies went to the bathroom before getting on the bus to the rafts.

"Sheena, who is this guy?" I said gruffly.

"Oh, just someone I met." Sheena shrugged as the "new guy" wasn't anyone special, but a decent companion for our outing.

"A little more detail, like maybe a name or do you even know his name?" I said, with frustration.

"Camille, back off of her already." Liza said.

"What?" I gawked.

"She's living her best life and having fun." Liza said.

"Thank you. Liza, I appreciate that."

"Don't thank me too much. Just try to find out his last name before you sleep with him." Liza giggled then we all busted out laughing, knowing that probably would not happen.

"Just be safe as you live your best life," Toni chimed in.

"Kasey, are you okay?" Liza asked noticing she wasn't joining the conversation.

"I'm okay. I am just glad to get to know you all."

"Glad you were able to come out with us." I said.

The water was amazing that day. We had to find a rhythm and learn to row together and we almost lost Kasey overboard, but we were having a great time. When we stopped for lunch, they sang happy birthday the Stevie Wonder version and Hunter, had some cupcakes.

"Thank all of you for coming out to spend time with me for my birthday. This was super fun and Hunter; I love the cupcakes."

"Glad you like them. It took me all night to get them right."

"You know he didn't bake those." Knowledge said. Everyone was cracking up.

"Man, you just going to throw me under the bus?"

"Dude, everyone knows you didn't do that." Josh jumped in.

We were having an awesome time. At the end, we brought keepsake pictures and sat around the fire talking. It was nice to mix our friends having a good time. That happened often, but as the years went on things changed. As we drove home, it was initially quiet. Then I had to ask about where the relationship was headed. We had talked about it several times, but we always maintained that we wanted to take things slow. I didn't want to push the issue, but I needed to know.

"Hunter, I had a great time."

"I'm glad Honeypot."

"I wanted to ask something." I could see him shifting as if he knew where the conversation was going.

"Honeypot look in my bag." I got the bag and discovered in the front pocket a card and little box. After reading the touching card and seeing peridot and diamond earrings he got for my birthday, I knew asking my question would be fine.

"Hunter, I am not seeing anyone else and I don't get the impression you are either. Are we an exclusive couple?"

"I already call you my girlfriend and have introduced you as such. That wasn't clear."

"We never said anything to each other."

"Well, I'm telling you now. There is no one else and I am taking you to meet my parents and siblings tomorrow."

"You are? Wait, when did your dad get in town?"

"Today. Wayne is going back to school the next day and they are driving him up. Junior year is upon him." I was excited the rest of the way home. He thought enough of me to introduce him to his family after intermingling our friends and agreeing that we were an official couple. This day felt so great and I kind of didn't want it to end. I wanted to just live in this moment. Of course, that was unrealistic and time never waits.

Hunter stayed at my house that evening. We got in the shower and at first, we were just showering. He took the washcloth from me and gently washed my back. He turned me around and we kissed, like never before. I felt breathless. We were embraced as we kissed and I could feel his penis, hard against my body. We got out, toweled off. He picked me up, carried me to my bed and gently laid me down. He kissed my lips, sucking on my tongue. I sucked his bottom lip as we continued to be gently lip locked. He disconnected our embrace and nibbled on my earlobe, kissing my neck as he gently rubbed my left nipple that became hard in between his thumb and index finger. He licked my nipple gently and began to suck my right breast while continuing to stimulate the left. I felt like the river running between my legs. The anticipation of what would happen next made me excited and anxious all at once. Then he stopped. He reached in his bag and pulled out the gold wrapper. I was nervous and breathing hard. Guess it was obvious to him, he smiled at me and picked up his phone and said, "Siri, play R and B playlist." Storm

(Forecass), Jamie Foxx began to play. I love this song. After the condom was on, he slid into my moist vagina and pumped in and out of me. I matched his movement and we began to go faster, as we kissed, occasionally making eye contact. He paused and we switched positions. Hunter had a way of making me feel comfortable with my body and sexiness. Holding with my waist, he moved in and out gently until he ended up laying me on my back and still giving me his dick. I felt his breath warm on my neck and then his tongue gently licked my earlobe. When we finally finished, or so I thought... he wiped my vagina and began to suck on my clit with vigor, he made me come several times.

"You okay?" He peered at me from between my legs.

"Mmmhuh." He gently licked my clitoris again and it sent shivers down my body. He did it a few more times until I pushed the top of his head slightly for him to stop. He came up next to me and pulled me close. The night as wonderful as the day and my mind was content as peace swept over us. We slept with the night air coming through the window over our heated skin. The fire was still smoldering between my legs as he gently kissed my lips.

The next morning, I felt drunk with sleep. He was facing me waiting for me to open my eyes. He was waiting to have more sex and dare I say make love to me. I smiled. I went to the bathroom to relieve my bladder and returned ready to go. I went in his bag getting another gold wrapped condom. I kissed him while rubbing his manhood gently to attention. When it was at full attention, I gently rolled it down his shaft. I mounted his penis and was moving at a rapid pace. His moans filled the air. His eyes tightly shut. We went at it like that for a while. I could tell he was holding on to that orgasm. I pounded into him with fervor, like my one mission in life was for him to ejaculate! When he did, I could feel the pressure deep inside me. Something happened that morning. A deep connection, that still binds us. At moments it is stronger than others but, I feel it and I know he does too.

Hunter

She made me nut like never before. When I pulled out, it was spilling. It was a feeling I will never forget. I know she felt it. Her eyes were filled with tears. We didn't say much, but I don't think it was necessary. We showered, dressed and rode quietly to my mother's house. About ten minutes away, she spoke.

"I'm nervous about meeting your family."

"Don't be. Just be yourself and it will be fine."

"Is my outfit okay?"

"I've never seen you like this."

"I'd like to make a good impression on your mom."

I'm not sure why she was so worried. I had zero concerns. If I did, it would not have happened. Taking a woman home to meet the family is huge. Camille was held in high regard. My sister was the only one I had concerns about. She tends to not warm up to people so quickly.

When we arrived, the family was milling around waiting for the food to be placed on the table. I introduced Camille and of course, Drew wasn't so polite.

"Oh, hi." She said, almost mumbling.

"I hear you are going to 11th grade."

"Yeah, so."

"Drew, stop being rude." I looked at her with an eye that said if you don't cut it out.

She stormed off to her room. I was about to go after her, when Camille stopped me.

"Ms. Douglas, may I?"

"Yes, of course." At the time, I didn't know what she said to Drew, but they came back down about ten minutes later.

"Ms. Douglas, thank you for my birthday cupcakes. They were delicious."

"No problem. It was my pleasure. I know if Hunter was asking for my help to impress you, then you were important to him."

Wayne thought he needed to weigh in on the conversation. "Let me guess, my big brother tried to pass them off as his own. Classic."

"Oh, so he has done this before?" Camille gave me a look that said we'd be discussing this further at a later date.

"Now, what kind of brother would I be Camille if I answered that?"

"I knew Hunter didn't do it on his own, although initially he tried to convince me."

"Wait, what are you trying to say?" She never ceased to amaze me; in front of my family she was coming at me.

"I'm saying, you can cook, but baking... A stretch." The table erupted with laughter.

My mother then jumped into the conversation and it took a turn in tone.

"What is it that you do young lady?" She said sounding like she was speaking to one of her students.

"I'm in school full time, getting a dual degree in social work and special education. I also run an after school during the school year and day camp in the summer."

"That sounds like a lot to manage." Dad, said.

"It sounds like you are doing a great job Camille. Especially if you have found time to entertain my son." Mom said and she smiled.

"Yes, it can be. I just try to stay organized and manage my time wisely. Maybe Drew could come and be a counselor next summer."

"Could I really?" She straightened up in her chair and looked between our parents for approval.

"Only if your grades continue to be good and you teach some music." I stated as a matter of fact.

"I would love that."

Camille had just won my family over. Drew was the hardest and I think she did a great job. Dinner was finished. As Wayne and Drew got up from the table. My mom asked, "Are you two not interested in dessert?"

Wayne said, "Mom, I promised Tyrik, CC and Jade I'd meet up with them before I leave for school tomorrow."

"Mom, I am going to chill. I will get some later." Drew said as she climbed the stairs to her room. My parents, Camille and I had more conversation.

"Please let me help clear the table Ms. Douglas."

"Why thank you." While the ladies were in the kitchen, my dad and I talked.

"She seems really nice, Son. Don't go messing it up."

"I really like her. She maybe "the one".

"Pace yourself."

"Dad, can I ask a personal question?"

"Sure, son."

"Do you love mom?"

"Of course, I do."

"I mean in a romantic way?" When my mom talks, I see how he looks at her. It happened during dinner this evening.

"Why are you asking?"

"Dad, you sometimes look at her in a way that says you still want to be with her. No disrespect."

"I often think about how things could have been different. But we are older and I think your mother is very comfortable with things the way they are."

"That does not mean you can't show her how you feel."

"Believe me, I think about it daily."

Shortly after, it was time to go. I went to take Camille home.

"So, inquiring minds want to know. What did you say when you went in the room with Drew?"

"I just told her that you will always be her brother and that I'd like to be friends. If she was willing, she would be making you happy and I know how important that is for her."

"Wow, that human behavior class you're taking is working."

"You got jokes, huh?" We laughed.

Camille

In those early days of our relationship our adventures and conversations seemed endless. He came home, looking tired. I had made dinner in an attempt to sit together and chat. I thought his favorite meal would help. Porterhouse steak, sweet and white mashed potatoes with asparagus. I had to enlist my mother-in-law's assistance for the asparagus. I kissed him. What was returned lacked passion.

"Hey babe, I made dinner. Wash your hands. I'm going to bring the wine and rolls to the table."

"In a minute." His tone harsh as if he was annoyed.

We sat and it was silent. I thought I would start the conversation.

"How was your day?"

"Busy as normal."

"I went to the doctor today."

"Oh yeah."

"I told her I was ready to get off the birth control. She said that people get pregnant rather quickly after."

"Oh yeah." His two-word answers were making it difficult for me to want to continue. It was hard enough having this conversation. It felt forced and I was getting very discouraged.

"I thought this was what you wanted. Was I wrong?"

"I want you to want it too."

"I do. I honestly feel ready."

"Well, good." More silence. We sat for a few minutes which felt like hours. It became deafening. I hit the remote to turn on some music.

"I'm meeting up with Knowledge and Josh after work tomorrow."

"Okay." After dinner, I showered, put on an enticing new piece of lingerie, in hopes to spark something in the bedroom. It had been about two weeks since he touched me. I attempted to pretend that Hunter had not lost interest. I loved my husband and wanted nothing more than to continue to build on what had begun five years past. I thought he had gone in his study to work, but I found him outside the other room. He didn't know but, often I found him in there staring... Looking hurt, disappointed and sometimes crying. I usually kept the door closed. I wanted to clear it out, but he refused to let me. He said he'd do it, but never did. I just went back to our bedroom and lay in bed. Two hours later, he came to bed. I was still awake.

"Hunter, I'd like to go on a weekend trip?"

"Oh really. To where?" The annoyed tone lingered in his voice. I didn't retreat.

"I found a deal on-line for Puerto Rico. We could use our frequent flyer miles. We could leave Thursday and come back Tuesday."

"My schedule is jammed packed."

"At least think about it. We could use a three-day weekend, that way we don't miss so much work." He rolled over and the conversation was over. That night, I cried myself to sleep. The silent tears that just run down your face. Thinking I was losing him, not knowing what else to do. I needed to talk to someone. I laid there looking at the ceiling. I miss the laughter. I miss the fun. The adventures. Then I thought of our first vacation.

It was after I graduated. We were off to Mexico! Margaritas, blue water and fun. I was super excited. We spent the most amazing four nights and five days frolicking around the resort. Funniest part of the trip was day four, we had breakfast and went paddle boating. Just something easy going, since we had already done snorkeling and jet skiing. I got in first, no big deal. I don't know what Hunter was doing, but somehow the boat tipped over and we both fell in. There were several people around and they gawked. Of course, we just had on shorts and tee shirts. We got out laughing and walked back to the room drenched. People just looked at us, I am sure trying to understand why we were soaking wet in our clothes. "I can't believe we fell in."

"Me either." I snickered.

"Well, there is nothing wrong with being a little wet is there?"

"Absolutely not." We began kissing and yet again giving ourselves one to another.

The last night of our stay we made love on the balcony. I was sitting, sipping wine when Hunter came in the room and walked onto the balcony.

"Hey babe." He took my glass and took a sip. He then leaned down and kissed my lips. He untied the robe I had on; it fell open. Hunter gently ran his fingers down my body… stopped… stood me up… we kissed. He turned me around and I held on to the railing, waiting and wanting to share myself with the man I loved. The gold wrapper fell to the balcony floor. He gently slid inside me. Moving in and out of me. I could hear the wetness from my yoni as our bodies came together. He held my breast and rubbed my nipples as he thrusted in and out. He let go and held my hips, as he continued to give himself to me, I met his thrust. There was very little sound from us, until an "ahhhhh" came from his lips. He had released. I straightened up and turned around to kiss his lips. We stood allowing our lips to embrace. Then Hunter took my hand and guided me inside, we laid on the bed, quietly holding one another. Our silence often communicated for us. This time it expressed satisfaction. Lately, quiet is almost explosive for us. He will not communicate with me, unless he has to.

Hunter

It had been rough at work and attempting to find solace at home just wasn't happening. I know she is trying hard to bring us closer, but I don't know how to interact the way we used to. The uncertainty about many things loomed over me. For about three months, I suspected Camille of cheating, but it turned out she wasn't and I felt stupid for thinking that. Knowledge kept telling me that she would never, that she loved me too much and I just kept digging for something that wasn't there. It got so bad that the last time I went spying, she was planning a surprise birthday gathering. I showed up home, drunk with our family and friends screaming, "SURPRISE!". I was beyond embarrassed. My father had come to town and my mother gave me a tongue lashing I will never forget.

"Son, I can't believe you even came home smelling like the barrel of whisky. Camille has been a pillar of strength while you are out getting drunk. I am embarrassed at your behavior and disappointed in you. You better come up with the best apology you can muster, not only to your wife, but her parents and us. I did not raise you to behave like a drunk buffoon." I just stood there. What could I possibly say to my mother? Camille just carried on with the party while I got in bed to sleep it off!

Apparently, after all the guests had gone home, Camille had a conversation with my boys.

"Knowledge, I don't know what to do anymore. It is so lonely. I am not sure if he even wants me anymore."

"He is hurting. I don't think he knows how to fix things." He replied.

"Sometimes, we aren't good at expressing our feelings." Josh lightly squeezed my hand.

"Guys, I appreciate you both for always looking out for him. I just feel like maybe it is time to let go."

Josh looked at her and said "Damn." I had gotten up to use the bathroom and overheard this conversation. It hurt to hear that my wife was unsure how I felt about her. I loved her with all my heart but, I realized my behavior was the antithesis of how I truly felt. Camille was trying to figure out if she should leave me. I loved her and wanted her to stay. I didn't want to lose her; I still didn't know how to make things right though. I went back to bed and fell asleep. I don't remember Camille coming to bed.

Today was the time to start something. When I woke, she was gone. I called. It rang several times, then voicemail...*You have reached Camille Douglas. Please leave your name, number and a brief message and I will return your call as soon as possible. Thank you and have a joy filled day.* She sounded so sweet. I called her cell, called the house, sent text to no avail. I went to meet up with Knowledge and Josh at our neighborhood watering hole after work.

"My man, you okay?" Knowledge said as I sat on the bar stool next to him.

"Yeah, I feel like an asshole though. Why didn't y'all give a heads up about the party?"

Josh laughed. "It was a surprise. If we told you, that would have defeated the purpose."

"I know but, still."

"Don't be mad auntie got in that ass." Knowledge laughed too.

"Don't remind me. I heard the conversation with Camille before you guys left. I can't believe she would consider leaving me."

They both looked at me and shook their heads. "What?" I said, feeling the heat rising all over my body.

"I love you, but you are thick." Knowledge said. "Fool, get it together before you lose the best thing that has ever happened to you. All couples have tough times, but they pass. All relationships require both parties to be intentional. You have to remain open, to conversation, to love and to deal with the hurt may come between you. I can't understand what you both have experienced with losing the baby, but this is where you have to be there for her. She physically went through it. I am not dismissing your feelings, but it is an outer body experience for you. It can't be just her; you have to participate in the process. Show up for your wife." Two hours had passed and we paid our bill and left. I kept checking my phone the entire time and still hadn't heard from her. I went home to find her on the couch looking at her phone.

"You couldn't return my calls or text messages." I know my tone was confrontational, but I was just worried.

"No."

"Why not?"

"I left my phone home."

"So, what happened when you got home?"

"I just walked in about five minutes before you."

"Could have text me Honeypot." It had been a long time since I called her that.

"I'm sorry you were worried. I am just seeing all the messages and missed calls."

"Where were you?"

"You really were worried, Hunter. Liza and I played hooky from work and went to Spa Castle."

"How was it?"

"Very relaxing. How was your day?"

"Hard. I couldn't concentrate because I didn't know where you were."

When I got in bed that night as usual, she was already in bed. I laid down and got close to hold her. She didn't resist or push me away. It was difficult at first because it had been way too long, but then, it felt good.

Camille

In the beginning, he held me all the time, with no hesitation. The night he proposed was one I will never forget. He took me away on a weekend vacation. He likes surprising me, at least he used to. We had gone to a resort in Pennsylvania. The first night there, we had dinner in the room. After dinner, he had masseuses come to the room and give us side by side massages. When they were done, sixty glorious minutes, Hunter and I created an invigorating happy ending. It was the first time we made love without reaching for the gold wrapper. He slowly slid inside my warm, wet and waiting vagina. A familiar song played from his phone. Storm (Forecass)! He always knew how to make me feel good all over. Hunter slowly pumped in and out. It felt amazing, a matching hand to glove. Our hands clasped into one another. Right at my ears. Again, the emotions ran so high that night, tears ran down my face. He whispered in my ear, "I love you." Hunter kissed my lips before I could respond. He sucked my left nipple gently grazing his teeth across. He lifted my right leg continuing to effortlessly move in and out of me, he played with my happy button. "Damn girl, you feel good." He kept going, making me remember why I fell in love with all of him. “Babe, I think I am going to … ahhhh. Fuck.” That must have excited him that I squirted while he was inside me. He kept going and put both my legs on his shoulders. Sometime after, it was his turn. He sounded like the King of the Pride Land, roaring the release of his swimmers. The first time anyone had done that. It felt good. We had moved to a new place in our relationship.

The next morning at brunch we went into the main dining hall and in front of strangers... he got down on one knee. "Camille Joy Pearson, I've spent the last year and a half loving you. I am asking that you allow me to do that for the rest of our lives. Will you be my wife?" I was crying and shaking my head. Everyone was clapping. It was an amazing feeling. I was going to be Mrs. Hunter Douglas. "How long have you been planning this?" I asked.

"A while, had to ask for some guidance from my mom and, of course, Liza."

"Yeah, I can imagine.”

“Honeypot, your middle name is Joy and I feel pure Joy when I am with you. It is no accident that your mother was moved to name you Joy.”

I verbally thanked him, but later I gave a physical thank you he'd never forget.
We returned to the room to shower and prepare for dinner after a long day of activities. We never made it to dinner. He stepped out the bathroom after showering with a towel wrapped around his waist. I took the towel gently patting him dry. I then put the towel back around his waist, hold on to each end. I sat on the bed and pulled him closer. Massaging his penis to attention with my mouth, expertly working my lips around it. Taking him in as far as I could go. This was head men dreamed of. I was going hard and I could tell he was going to release by the grunting and tight grip on my shoulders. I wasn't ready for him to enable his swimmers to escape. I stopped and stood up push him back slightly and made him lay down on the bed. I sat atop his rock-hard erection. We were going at it hard and quick. We weren't talking, there was some cussing, ass slapping, grunts and moans. When he couldn't hold back any longer, he held my butt tightly in the palms of his hands to get me to stop movement. We then collapsed. Intertwined. After trying to get our breath back, we started up all over again. I miss days like that, we had seamless sexual encounters. Filled with lust, romance and love! Intimacy inside and outside the bedroom. Those are the memories I keep close to my heart. I knew the man I loved was still there, he just needed to find his way back to me.

Hunter

It was a Saturday morning and I smelled food from the kitchen. I went down and she had a spread that was amazing. Bacon, eggs, home fries, 7- up biscuits, fruit.

"Good Morning, how did you sleep?"

"Good, how long have you been up?" I gently kissed her on her cheek.

"Since five. I went for a run, showered, came back and here is breakfast." She was looking good. Glowing in fact.

"It smells really good."

"Who is eating all this food?"

"Me, you, maybe Drew and Kathy."

"You should stop cooking for them all the time."

"Hey, we all needed home cooked food in college. Drew is my sister too. I rather know she is eating good food, instead of junk."

"Okay, okay." I felt the need to talk. It was so hard to get the words out. I was stalling by eating. As usual, she started the hard conversation.

"It was nice to have you hold me last night."

"Honeypot, I want to work this out."

"Well we can go see the therapist." Why was she suggesting someone being in our business, again? I am not feeling therapy.

"No, I want to do it on our own."

"Hunter, it is sometimes better to have a third neutral party. It won't be a colleague. I will ask my officemate to refer us to someone who is good, I trust her judgement." I got where she was coming from and in the years we had been together, she never once used her therapeutic techniques on me. I trusted her professional opinion. I was too afraid to admit it though. Before I could say anything else, the doorbell rang.

"I will go. On one condition." I said as I walked toward the door.

"That is?"

"We go on that trip you were talking about." I got to the door and the noise brigade strolled in. Drew's roommate, Kathy became a permanent fixture at our family gatherings. She played violin. She and Drew became good friends and she had become part of our family.

"Hello Ladies, how are you?"

Drew kissed me on the cheek. "We are good and hungry."

"Hunter, thanks for having us over."

"It smells good in here." Kathy said.

"I didn't invite you two over here. That is my wife's doing."

"Hunter, shut up." Drew said. "Sis, please get this dude."

I went back to eating my food, but shortly the girl talk was too much and I went into the den.

Camille

I was in shock and awe. He agreed to go to therapy. This has to be the answer I have been praying for. I had been asking God if we were to stay married or move on, especially after the stunt he pulled for his surprise birthday gathering. I needed God to speak to me in a way that I could understand. I was worried that his answer would be to move on. I went to the bedroom and sat. I was so happy, I wanted to talk to my mother.

"Mom, how are you?"

"I'm good baby, the question is, how are you? I know that things have been difficult and from the looks of things at the party, Hunter isn't doing that great."

"Today is a good day. He agreed to therapy."

"Glad to hear. I have been praying for you both. Talking it out will hopefully be helpful."

"I want to do brunch tomorrow. Are you available?"

"For you daughter, always. Are you going to ask Lorraine to come?"

"I didn't think about that, but that is a good idea. I will call her and ask."

"Sounds like a plan. Where and what time Camille?"

"1pm at Ricardo's Steakhouse." I go back down to find little food left and a conversation about the latest plan cooked up to enjoy graduation. Drew had already been asked to tour with several orchestra's and a few artists as well. For now, she was playing for their church and waiting to make a final decision. Kathy was planning on going back home to California.

"Sis, sorry to eat and run. Food was amazing." Drew said holding on to the last piece of bacon.

"Yes, Camille, thanks for always opening your home to us." Kathy said.

The girls said their goodbyes and the overwhelming need to cry happened.

"Honeypot, what's wrong?" This was the second time, he called me by the nickname given so long ago. When I asked why Honeypot. He told me I was his gold at the end of the rainbow.

"I'm happy and sad. I can't believe the girls are all grown up. I'm just thinking about where..." He quickly cut me off.

"We are going out. I'm going to shower." We get in the car and ended up at Brooklyn Boulders. We had not been in such a long time. Suddenly, things began to change. I don't really know what clicked, but it was good. It wasn't the same, but we were working toward change. Instead of going home, we went and did a little shopping and then to the Brooklyn Marriott and got a room. We showered, dressed and went out to O'Keefe's for drinks and bar food. The young couple that fell in love had returned. We went back to the room and made love, had sex and straight up fucked all over that hotel room.

"Damn girl! You making up for lost time."

"That isn't possible, but I'm taking advantage of the moment."

"Look, I'm sorry. I know I allowed my insecurity to cloud my judgement, but it has been hard." I don't know if it was the alcohol, but he broke down and cried. "I was so hurt after our loss. I was angry at you and it was misdirected. I was really angry with myself. I love you Honeypot and I want to start fresh. I know we can't erase the past, but I am hoping to build on our future." That night was a start to something special, but I knew it was just that, a start. I needed to call and cancel brunch with the moms.

The morning after yielded two very hung-over people, with giggles. We drove home discussing what we both wanted moving forward. I got quiet.

"I wasn't ready. You know, to try again."

"I understand, I was being selfish." It has been almost two years now.

"Babe, it felt like my fault. Even now, I feel like there is something I should have known or done so we wouldn't lose our baby."

"Camille, it was not your fault." I saw the sincerity in his eyes when he uttered those words.

Hunter

While I thought of the possibilities of things getting better. I was taken back to where things fell apart. It was fall and a chill was in the air. We just returned from a five-day cruise. Camille had experienced sea sickness on previous trips, but not quite like this. We made the most of our trip. She would be sick most mornings until the afternoon, but in the evening. She was fine.

"Honeypot, I think you should go to the doctor when we get back. Especially if this continues on land."

"I'm sure it will stop then." When we docked that afternoon, she looked wiped out. We jumped in a cab and got home as quickly as possible. She slept for what seemed like an eternity. I called her mother. "Mrs. P, how are you?"

"Fine Hunter. How was the trip? It was pretty good, but Camille's motion sickness was really bad."

"Really? How is she now?"

"She's been asleep for the last two hours. I've never seen her like this."

"Hunter, I'm coming down. Let her sleep." Mrs. P apparently called my mom because they kind of showed up at the same time. They kissed me, handed me some bags and went up to our bedroom. They told me to stay downstairs. I was worried, but attempted to calm myself. I looked in the bags they left on the counter. There was food, food and more food. They must think we don't shop. Finally, they all came down.

I stared at them waiting for someone to say something. "Well." I said in frustration.

"Hunter, it never dawned on me, but you are going to be a daddy." I ran and picked her up off her feet. I was ecstatic about being a parent. A child with the woman I loved, what more can a man ask for? Our mothers hugged as they looked on at us hugging. We couldn't hide our excitement. They cooked us dinner and left for the evening, barking instructions. "Camille, please make an appointment with the doctor in the morning. Mrs. P. said.

"Yes, honey, you need to know how far along you are and get your prenatal vitamins." My mom said.

It had been 36 weeks of pregnancy. She looked so tired and wasn't sleeping well. Those months of vomiting were awful and then it wasn't. She had finally stopped getting sick and was enjoying her pregnancy. I was a little uncomfortable, because I didn't always know how to be there for her. There were several baby showers, we decorated the room for our child to be and did all the things to prepare for the hospital. She had already been having some contractions. We went in for her weekly checkup, hoping the doctor would tell her she could stay. Immediately, during the ultrasound, I knew something was wrong. I didn't hear the heartbeat as I normally would. Then they started asking Camille a bunch of questions. It sounded like white noise to me. I was holding her hand. When did you last feel the baby move? The doctor finally confirmed what I knew. I tried to stay calm for her. I called her mother first.

"Mrs. P., you need to come to the hospital." By this time, Camille was hysterically crying.

"Hunter, is everything okay?"

"No ma'am." I felt my body temperature rising and my tears forming clouding my vision. "Can you call my mother and ask her to come too?"

"Of course." She hung up and I went back to attempting to console my wife.

Camille had to deliver this baby. I was PISSED OFF! I couldn't fix this for her. How was she going to deliver our baby who had gone already? I was devastated.

When her parents arrived, only her mother went in the room. I walked out for a minute and found her father sitting with red eyes. He went to hug me and I yelled over and over. "No heartbeat." I collapsed in his arms. He just hugged me as if I was his own.

I had to get myself together to return to the room. It took a trip to the bathroom for me to wash my face. It was an hour later, when it was time to push, both our mothers were in the room. I was on one side and Mrs. P was on the other side of her. As she pushed, tears fell from her eyes. She pushed several more times. Then, labor was over, but there were no cries. **COMPLETE SILENCE!** As suspected, it was a boy. We named him Rhys Hunter.

Those next few days I was flooded with emotions and memories I had shelved, but resurfaced. I didn't know how to help my wife? I couldn't even help me.

Camille

What was supposed to be the best day of my life was the worst day. After hearing the doctors say that there was "no heartbeat," I lost it. I became hysterical. After I finally calmed down, they induced my labor. In about forty-five minutes, it was time to push. I felt the baby's head crowning.

"Nurse Tiffany, I think it's time."

"Let me check." She said. After taking a quick look she said, "You are right. Let me get the doctor." I couldn't believe I had to deliver this baby.

In just a few pushes, Rhys was born still. My mother-in-law went with him and the nurse to get cleaned up. While they did that, I delivered the placenta. Then the tears came again. I couldn't stop. My mother held me and Hunter walked away to see Rhys. They had asked if we wanted to hold him prior to delivery. Of course, I needed to see him, touch him, talk to him and hold him. All that time, and now he was gone. Nurse Tiffany handed him to me, wrapped in a blanket.

"Hunter, honey, you want to hold him?"

"Yeah." Tears were falling from his eyes. Our mothers had stepped out along with Nurse Tiffany to give us some time.

"Baby, this hurts so bad. Why us?" I said to Hunter.

"Honeypot, I don't know." By this time, the entire family was there. My father was able to catch a flight. He hugged me and I just cried. They stayed with us until it was time to let Rhys go. Once they took him, I cried so hard. Nurse Tiffany was sweet and help us prepare to switch from the birthing room to where we would stay. Once we were settled, Hunter left. No one knew where he had gone. Our parents and Drew had gone home. Liza and Sheena had dropped by and he still had not returned. I called him on his cell and he didn't answer.

It was two hours later before I saw Hunter again. He returned with food.

"Hunter, why didn't you just say you were going to get food?"

"I don't know."

"Well, I appreciate it."

"No problem." He appeared so broken. I understood or so I thought. My husband had been keeping a secret from me.

"I got burgers and fried with milkshakes."

"It smells good. That didn't take two hours, did it?"

"I needed to think and get air." I dropped the conversation.
We ate our dinner in virtual silence.

****

When we left the hospital, I felt so cheated and empty. Walking in with a swollen belly to leave with nothing. We created keepsakes, but no baby. This had to be the worst feeling ever. The feeling of emptiness on the inside and our hands literally empty. **NO BABY!** We got home and my mother was there. She had prepared brunch, but I could not eat. I just went to get in the bed. I was so overwhelmed with emotions. Hunter eventually came in the room, but he didn't ask if I needed anything or how I was doing, he just laid in the bed, silently. I didn't know what to make of his behavior. It was hard because I wanted us to communicate, but I didn't want to push.

About two weeks after we had gotten home and were trying to find our new normal, we had a vicious argument, one that was hard to forget. He was saying things that did not quite make sense. He was yelling about child loss, but couldn't have been about us and our son.

"I feel so guilty Camille, like God is punishing me."

"Babe God isn't punishing you." Trying to reassure him that losing Rhys was no one's fault.

"Camille, he is. How could this happen to me again?" This questioned puzzled me because I didn't know what he meant by again.

"Hunter, what are you talking about, again?"

"When I was 16 years old, my girlfriend, Keisha got pregnant and she had an abortion." I was dumfounded. Did my ears deceive me? Did he say he got a girl pregnant? There was an abortion. I then wondered what other things he had not told me. I thought we shared everything.

"And you never told me about that?"

"There wasn't anything to tell. I hardly ever think about it. It never seemed like the right time to bring it up or necessary. Besides Keisha and I broke up the summer after senior year. We never spoke again."

"And again, you didn't think this something you should share with me?"

"Honestly, I didn't think there would be a reason to share."

"I'm your wife, your friend. We have shared so much; I just feel like at some point this would have been on the share list." This was where things turned left.

"Oh my God! IT WASN'T YOUR BUSINESS!"

"None of my business, none of my business." I felt like crying, but I was too mad. "I AM YOUR WIFE!" I yelled. "You should be able to tell me anything, past or present. How can I be there for you if I don't have all the information?"

"Who said I needed you?" Those words stung. It was as if I had been attacked by bees. I walked away before I said something more or he did. I just couldn't deal with that, more hurt. I felt like I could not breathe and needed to get air. Just get away. I lost my son and now my husband was expressing that he did not need me. In my rational mind, I knew that was his hurt talking, but all the same it felt like fifty daggers coming at me. Cutting through my flesh, leaving me like mincemeat. There were so many emotions in the room that it couldn't all be contained. I left after that and went to my mother's house. I needed to be loved, hugged and told that all would be well.

About two months after, I was tired of crying and needed to do something. I joined a support group. He blamed them for me wanting to get rid of Rhys' things. I just wanted to sell the pieces and donate the money to charity. I needed to have a fresh start. He wouldn't hear of it and the distance between us grew. I suggested we both go to therapy, together. He said I was crazy. We argued often. I cried which felt like daily either about the loss of our son or the loss of our relationship. We lost our closeness to tragedy. He got angry because I got back on birth control. I needed to heal before traveling that road again and we were in a rocky place. I had so many concerns because he wasn't addressing his feelings. He was attempting to move right past them again. Everyone said to give him time. Then the excessive drinking. I was cleaning up vomit more than I cared to. Caring for an adult baby. He wasn't a baby; he was a grown man. It was hard to keep it together and I needed support.

"Liza, can I come stay the night?"

"You know you can."

"Can you make chili?"

"Yeah. The kids are at their grandma's. Josh won't bother us."

"See you in a few." I got in the car and left to Liza's. I tried to keep my cool, not cry. The tears came anyway. When I got there. I parked and just sat in the car. Ten minutes later I got out. Liza was at the door.

"I wondered how long you were going to sit there."

"Sorry. Just gathering my thoughts."

"Let's eat." The chili was good. I didn't speak much.

"Liza, he's really not getting better. I'm not sure if I should stay or go."

"Is he hurting you?"

"No, never touched me once, but has been destructive in a drunk state."

"Keep praying. If you love him, stay. As long as he isn't hurting you verbally or physically."

"It is hard."

"Marriage isn't easy. I know people want to portray it as such, but it's isn't. It makes matters worse that we now have social media. Everyone only shows all the beautiful things. No one is showing the tragedy and hurt they are going through. Very few people being transparent. Josh and I have had our tough times too. The themes were different, but it was just as difficult, you know."

"Thanks for being honest."

"That's what sister-friends are for. Let's pray. Dear Heavenly Father, we thank you for all your blessings big and small. God, we come asking for healing. We know God that you can do anything, but fail. I pray specifically for Hunter and Camille send them comfort and blanket them in your love. Allow Hunter to be open to what you are trying to say them in this season and allow him to be able to communicate better with his wife, Camille. Remind him of the love he has for her. We end this prayer with thanksgiving in Jesus name, Amen."

"Amen." After Liza prayed for Hunter and I, we drank and talked for hours. At three in the morning, we finally went to bed. The next morning, Josh and Liza took me to breakfast at Cracker Barrel. That felt good. Food cooked at a restaurant, but felt like home.

Hunter

She was gone for hours. Where was she? Why didn't she come home? She walked in the door like things were okay.

"Hey."

"Where you been?" I was waiting for the lies. I knew she was out here cheating on me.

"I stayed at Liza's. You were drunk. I figured you would sleep it off."

"Sure, you were there." That response was dripping with sarcasm.

"Where else would I go? I didn't want our parents to be privy to all the nonsense."

"Nonsense. That's how you see this?" She gave me a blank stare.

"You were probably with some other dude." Maybe, I should not have said that. Damn, I couldn't take it back.

"WOW!" She walked away and it was warranted. I am not sure where she was, but once I said it, I knew I shouldn't have accused her of that. I felt small and careless. My wife was in pain, I wasn't supportive. I just didn't know how to stop being an ass. My cell phone rang breaking into my thoughts.

"Hello." I wasn't really in the mood to talk.

"Dude, you are going to lose a good woman with your stupid shit."

"What are you talking about Josh?"

"I would never get in the middle, but Cam was here with us last night and I see her trying to hold it together. You better pull it together before you lose her."

I didn't know what to say except. "Thanks." That was the hardest conversation and it was so short. Here I was accusing my wife of stepping out and she just needed to be with friends. Now I felt worse.

Our Therapy

"The behavior I displayed was inexcusable." Hunter said.

"What do you want moving forward?" I said.

"I'd like to show my wife support and let go of the past. Try to move forward." At least he gave a clear answer. Most people say I don't know and while they don't it doesn't help to move the therapeutic process forward. I needed to hear how her husband's behaviors were impacting her.

"Camille, how did Hunter's actions feel?"

"As if he did not care. As if he didn't trust me. It hurt."

When the tears started falling, I was reminded of an older version of myself, heartbroken by loss of a child.

I continued trying to get past the countertransference I was experiencing in this moment.

"Hunter, why did you keep that part of yourself from Camille?"

"Honestly, I didn't think it mattered. It was so long ago. I don't even speak to the girl it happened with."

"Do you think you dealt with it initially?" I asked.

He sat. Silent. Quiet. Then, he finally spoke.

"No, not at all. I was seventeen. Just went on with life as it was. I feel like losing my son brought that old memory back."

"You always say, "my son". Is it hard to use the name you and Camille chose for him?"

"I guess. I mean yes."

"Sometimes naming the thing that hurt can help with healing. In this case, saying Rhys's name. Or do you think it makes it all the more real for you?"

"It is hard to say his name. I don't get to know who he is. I had plans to play with him, teach him things, impart wisdom and it was all taken away." Hunter's head was in his hands.

"Camille, I see you shaking your head. What are your thoughts at this moment?"

"I wish he had told me. Trusted me enough to share. Things happen before you meet your spouse, I understand that, but knowing about some of those experiences also helps to understand the person they have become. Losing our son was the worst imagined thing to happen. I feel like the world was thrown off of its axis. I couldn't imagine after all that time, carrying our child that he would be taken from us."

"Thank you, Camille, for sharing. Where are you both in the thoughts about trying again to have children?"

"I got off the birth control a month ago." Camille said.

"I'm willing to try again. I just don't want our last experience to hinder our ability to enjoy the next pregnancy." Hunter said as he looked down at his hands.

"What, if anything did you do with Rhys' things?"

"We sold them." Hunter said.

"How was that for you both?"

"It was hard, but we were able to raise money to assist pregnant teens in a shelter and donated the crib to a young lady who had just gotten her apartment. I felt good about it and moving forward."

"How did that make you feel, Hunter?"

"I was glad we could help out, but I definitely felt sad about it. It was like saying goodbye all over again. I did keep one thing that I had custom made for him. I wanted to have something to remember. I don't want him to be forgotten."

"Why do you think he will be forgotten?" I said.

"Well, I am not sure. It's just. The baby that was aborted was not really remembered and I don't want this to be like that.

"Hunter, that is impossible. I would never forget our son. I will always celebrate him. Rhys is part of our lives." Camille was passionate when she said these words. "I carried him with me for so long and the separation was hard, especially because it was finite physical separation. I still have phantom kicks. I could never forget our baby."

"How has the relationship improved?"

Camille answered. "I feel like he is taking more time to care for me and us. We have taken a trip. We have been eating at the table which is fostering more conversation."

Hunter then spoke. "I feel like we are more at ease with one another. I feel like I am not assuming things, I am asking questions. When I need a little space, I can ask for it."

"I'm going to suggest that we meet every other week. I think you two have made progress and have the tools to keep going."

They gathered their things to leave. When they left, I sat and thought about my princess that I also lost shortly after she was born prematurely. People do not realize how often pregnancy and infant loss take place. It is only until people are open about it that others will not feel shamed to silence.

Camille

Our anniversary was coming and I had a surprise for him. October 13, we pledged our love to one another. This year, I made arrangements for dinner. After dinner at River Park we walked along the water. Away from the crowds of people. I gave him a card. He opened it and his face was puzzled.

"Congratulations? I'm confused." He looked at me like, what's the joke.

"Keep reading."

He read aloud. *"To My Husband, I know we have had some rough times, but I see that we have re-committed ourselves to having a better relationship. A more in tune marriage. On this day, I want to congratulate you because our family is about to grow. I love you more than words can express. HoneyP.*

"Does this mean? Are you really? How do you feel?" I attempted to answer, but he was firing questions.

"Hunter take a breath. I just found out; I am only 6 weeks. We should keep this to ourselves for now."

"Of course."

"There is one more thing."

"There is more. What else could there be?"

"Yeah, we are going to have triplets."

"Really? Three? I can't believe it. How? Multiples don't even run in our families." He was beaming with pride.

"The doctor thinks it has something to do with the changes from getting off the birth control."

Days like this I cherished the hellos, the goodbyes, the closeness, the rekindled relationship. We renewed our vows. An impromptu ceremony. God, a minister and us.

Part 3

Sarah & Kristen

We Lay in Silence

Sarah

I have been waiting so long to hold Kristen, kiss her lips and let her know how much I'm into her. I have been attracted to her since we met. Today was not the first time she made me feel all warm inside. I saw her and was blown away by her earthy look. She wore makeup, but just enough to enhance. She was petite, caramel skinned, had a cute haircut, a nice round rump and breasts I thought about suckling all too often.

I had to be refined in the moment because I was in an Education Equality Coalition meeting. Today's focus, raising parent awareness about the inequality of student education. Kristen was a third-grade teacher and had been for eight years. She was intelligent and was truly dedicated to the children of her community. Her principal recognized her leadership skills and asked that she get her administrative license. She is currently working toward that after completing two masters. I personally feel tired just thinking of all the hard work she has put in. After the first meeting, I knew I wanted to connect with her. Today, I had to throw caution to the wind. I gave her my card after having a five-minute conversation.

The coalition meets once every other month. It was about a week after the last meeting, I was excited to hear from Kristen. I felt like I was in high school again and you got the message in your locker from the person you like. The first correspondence was via email. Very simple, yet I felt excited.

Sarah,
It was good to chat with you after the meeting last week. I would love to talk more. Maybe we could have drinks or dinner sometime.
Best,
Kristen

Kristen Jones, M.Ed, LMSW
Administrative Intern
3rd Grade Teacher

Marcus Garvey Elementary School
123 148th Street
New York, NY 10002
Phone 646.566.8888 ext 15911
Fax 646.566.7888

As I sat in my office, I could not believe my eyes. I was overwhelmed with thoughts of spending time with her and this had made my day. I didn't want to seem so eager, so I waited for about a half an hour before I responded.

Kristen,
Nice to hear from you and I am usually free after 6pm if you would like to meet up after work.
Sarah

Sarah Eckstien, LMSW
Horn Street Services
1913 7th Avenue
New York, NY 10000
Phone: 212.813.4092 ext. 122
Fax: 646.707.1979

Making a move I called Kristen at work. A bit nervous, I called about 3:15pm on Thursday. I got the impression that she never left work early. The office answered and after asking to speak to her, I was put through to her classroom. When she answered, I was delighted to hear her voice.

"Hello, Ms. Jones speaking."

"Kristen, it's Sarah."

"Hello. How are you?"

"I'm well and would like to know if you are free tomorrow." I was praying she would say yes and wasn't busy.

"I would love to. Especially since this week has been rough. Where should we meet?"

"I can come get you from work. I have to see a client at a school near you."

Kristen

This woman has been eyeing me since day one. She thinks I haven't noticed. I'm a teacher; my life is about being observant. I thought she was attractive as well. Standing at 5 feet 4 inches, I instantly felt even shorter when we got face to face, I realized she was at least five-seven, thin, dark features, jet black hair cut into a bob that framed her face.

After meeting Sarah and having a short conversation, I was taken with her. She was very intelligent and had so many positive thoughts on how we could make forward movement. Initially my skepticism was in high gear. Why was this white woman into this coalition, benefiting kids of color? It didn't appear that she had children. Was this some white guilt thing? I'd hoped she didn't have a savior complex. I did not get her angle at first. Then I started to see a woman who understood privilege and just wanted equality for children. I felt that this was a beautiful thing and it made me more interested. I didn't know what tipped her off that I was not straight, but I'm glad she was aware.

I was happy that we had set a date to do dinner and have more conversation. I was excited, but it was nervous excitement. Would Sarah be what I had created in my mind or would she be another imposter? You know, when you see the best foot forward side, but then you get the ugly truth? I had no time for games. While I was not looking to get married, I was interested in having something solid. Things were difficult with managing the certification courses and caring for my aging mother. The good part is that my Auntie Jan was the best support I could have ever asked for. She didn't have children of her own. She was married once, but that ended. Uncle Bert aka Herbert Shepherd II was still good to us. Apparently, some people make better friends. If you saw the two of them together you would never know they were not married.

The morning we were going out, I was so excited I woke up extra early and did some work for my class. I had an assignment that needed to be completed.

Then I dreaded at the moment, *what to wear*. It had to be work appropriate but, make me look fabulous for later. I settled on a blue and cream and plaid pencil skirt, cream button up shirt and blue kitten heeled shoes. As I am getting to the door, the phone rang. I answered.

"Hello."

"Krissy, it's auntie."

"Hey, I'm trying to get out the door. Can I call you later?"

"Honey, I just wanted to ask if you were going by your mother's this Saturday."

"Yes, I am."

"Good. I will text you a list of items to get her."

"Okay, Love you. Talk soon."

"Love you too."

Sarah

As promised, I met Kristen at the school. We went for dinner and drinks at Benny's Burritos. The frozen drinks are sublime. My favorite is the Black Flower. It is a mix of margarita and sangria; its color is a lush purple on top and white on bottom. During dinner we were getting to know one another, she was pretty open.

"Where is your family from?" She asked.

"Upstate, Schenectady."

"Is that close to Albany?"

"Yeah." I got pretty quiet and in my own head. I hated it up there. It wasn't exactly the most peaceful place. But Kristen interrupted my thoughts.

"You okay? You looked pretty far away."

"I'm good. Where did you go for grad school?"

"I graduated from Hunter for both degrees. When I finished undergraduate school, my aunt and my mother made it clear that I needed to get my masters right away. I never planned for two, but I ended up going back for a second masters."

"One was enough for me. Licensing for the MSW is like torture and extremely expensive."

"You are right about that."

"I actually am at Horn Street to get my clinical hours."

"Ahhhh. Now I see."

"See what? In it for the money. Private Practice."

"Not in it for the money, but I would like to have a private practice so I am able to get my debt down. Columbia is expensive."

"In that case, I get it. How was Columbia?"

"I think I was annoyed with the amount of people of color that were not in the room."

"That bad huh."

"Worse than that bad." We laughed. "Then on top of that it was frustrating to interact with white folk who were clueless. You have to be aware so that you can do the work."

"Exactly, things won't change until people of privilege, white people speak up about the injustice around us."

"Right."

There was some silence.

I asked, "How is your burrito? I personally love a good bowl."

"I love this burrito; it is like happiness and gladness in every bite. All of my favorites wrapped together, chicken, cheese, guacamole, black beans and rice."

"What a way you have with words. You actually are selling that burrito. I almost want one." I was loving the conversation. The down to earth persona was ringing true. "Sarah, what's your favorite old school movie?"

"Don't laugh, I have two. Sixteen Candles and Pretty in Pink."

She stared at me for a minute and then laughed. "What? I had a crush on Molly Ringwald. What about you?"

"Shaft. My dad was a fan."

"I would have never guessed that, but I like Shaft too."

"Really, how did you end up watching 70s Blaxploitation movies?

"A friend in high school. Jeff and I would hang at his house and he loved those movies. It was my escape from my home life. Jeff's mom would allow me to stay for dinner often and my favorite was when she would make rice krispie treats. They were the best. She would even let me help. Ms. Evelyn was sweet." We sipped the last of our drinks.

"Do you and Jeff still keep in contact?" She asked.

"Yeah, he is still my best friend."

"He lives in Georgia though. We don't see each other often, but we talk."

After paying the check we wandered further down to Pieces on Christopher Street. As we sat at the bar talking her hand landed on my leg. We were now on drink two and her inhibitions were way down. Womanizer came on and she got up and started dancing. It was so sensuous, like a burlesque show. Her arms moved, her hips swayed, her movements fluid. She captured the attention of the small crowd. When she finished her performance, I ordered our third drink.

As we sipped, I could see that we needed to get going because we had our fill of alcohol. We walked outside into the crisp night air and plenty of yellow cabs were going by. I hailed one pretty quickly and we headed to my place and before the cab could pick up momentum she was out of her bra. Then unexpectedly she grabbed my hand and put them in her folds of flesh. Wait! What! No panties! Oh man, this was not what I expected. Her vagina was so wet. I was excited to begin this intense sexual experience, but it was the first date and I didn't want her to regret it in the morning.

We got to my house; I paid the cabbie and guided her into my building. We got into the apartment and she asked to go to the bathroom. After she emerged, I took her to my bed, removed what was left of her clothing. I kissed her slowly and passionately, exploring her tongue. Her kisses were gentle, her lips were soft. I could taste the residual alcohol. Moved down to her plump breasts. I finally lowered my mouth to her warm center. I slowly licked her clit and sped up, giving her my fingers. She grinded on my fingers and I sucked harder on her clit until she climaxed, gave in to the vigor of my tongue and collapsed.

"How do you feel?" I whispered in her ear.

"Relaxed." Just like that. She was sleeping.

In the morning, I woke up to a smiling face that was glowing in the sunlight coming through the window. I didn't even say good morning, gave her the lightest kiss on her lips and trailed my tongue down her neck and through her breast, swirling around her navel as she arched her back up to meet my mouth with her sweet vagina. I started out fast and then slowed down to tease her. She gently grabbed my head and said 69. We maneuvered into the position and brought each other to ecstasy to each other; I was feeling her skills. She came first, her body shuddering.

"Well, good morning, how did you sleep?"

"Too good, I woke up and had to look around. Then realized where I was. I need coffee."

"How about coffee and breakfast?"

"YUMM, bring it on. I feel like I never ate last night."

I went in the kitchen, got the coffee brewing, made bacon omelets with green peppers and onions and toast.

"Sarah from Schenectady."

"Mmmhuh." I hoped she wasn't about to ask more about my family. They are completely vile and heinous.

"Have you traveled much?"

"I actually went with Jeff and his family on a cruise prior to leaving for college. Then while in college, I did a couple of Spring Break trips. Other than that, not as much as I would like to. What about you?"

"I did a study abroad in Seville, Spain, which is how I really learned to hone my Spanish speaking skills. It has come in handy. Thanks to my Auntie Jan and her ex-husband, I have actually gone to lots of places in the Caribbean via cruise ships. One of my favorite vacation memories was a trip with my parents to Canada. It was so cool to see Niagara Falls." After talking for a while, Kristen decided to go. I was hoping she would stay all day and hang in with me.

"Sarah, I have to get going, I've got to get some school work done and take care of a few errands." There was a pause as if she was thinking of how to word her next statement. "Let's catch a movie or something tonight." Inside I was doing a happy dance, but attempted to respond calmly.

"That sounds good, let's do the movies and then I can make you dinner."

"If it was as good as breakfast, I'm in."

"Are you allergic to anything?"

"Not food, just seasonal allergies." We said our goodbyes and I was anticipating our reconnection.

Kristen

The vibes were great. I usually don't do sex on a first date, but I could not resist allowing her to take control and make me climax. It had been such a long time since I had been on a date. It was nice to be treated like I was the only one in someone's universe and she wanted to spend more time with me. I did not know where this was going, but I was enjoying it. When I reached home, Karen had called my house like four times. Not to mention, the countless text messages on my cell. I broke up with this girl over eight months ago and she still would not leave me alone. My ex Karen and I met, started dating and then it got weird. She was possessive and verbally abusive. She would tell me that my hair was nappy and that no one wanted to see a dancer who was second rate. She would try to get me to get weaves and wigs. I wanted nothing more to do with her, but she kept calling and texting. I continued to ignore the calls and messages and never responded. My friends kept telling me to change my number, but I thought that was just ridiculous to have to do. Lately, I started to think maybe they were right. The messages were more aggressive and I really didn't need any more stress.

I took care of my schoolwork, several lesson plans for the upcoming week. I finally was able to shower and ran to see my mother. She was not doing well and it was very hard for me to deal with. I would go to her house and make sure she had all she needed.

"Hey mom, how have you been?"

"Just fine honey."

"Are you sure? You don't look fine."

"I'm feeling better. Even went for a walk this morning."

"Well look at you being active."

"I got all the things you had on the list."

"What about my medications?"

"Mom, they are all there on the counter. I even put them in the pill packs for the week. Do you need me to do anything else?" I wanted to make sure she did not have much to contend with.

"I don't think so. Jan left food for me to have in Tupperware. Thanks Krissy. I love you."

"Love you mom. I am going to get myself going. Call me or auntie if you need anything." I had cleaned the bathroom and straightened up her living room as well. There were some things that were more difficult for my mom to manage. I was exhausted after, but wanted to see Sarah. We met at 42nd street and I brought a change of clothes, just in case. I know, it was presumptuous.

We arrived at the theater simultaneously. We decided to see Shaft, since we established over dinner last night that we had both seen the previous one. As I approached the line, a middle -aged white couple walked in front of me.

"Excuse you."

"Were you on line? We didn't see you." The lady responded.

"How could you not see her?" Sarah responded. Then the lady's disposition changed.

"Oh, I am so sorry." The lady then said.

We got our tickets and made our way to the theater.

"Microaggressions piss me off." Sarah said.

"At least you don't have to experience them."

"I have, but they are usually about being a woman."

"Well imagine having to have double the *ism* when you are a woman and black."

"I hear you. I can't imagine, but I see you and I hear you.

We got our seats and Sarah went to get snacks. When she came back, I asked, "Did you leave anything for the other movie goers?"

"Well, I was a little hungry. Okay, so I went overboard."

"Let's see what you got here. Popcorn, soft pretzels, soda, MnMs, chicken fingers, curly fries and sour patch kids. I think you covered all bases for sure. Did you get ketchup and barbeque sauce?"

"I did." We started laughing. While we watched the screen, we ate the snacks. When we had our fill of snacks, she held my hand. There was an electricity between us and it felt like it was 1000 volts or maybe I was completely horny. Either way, I was hoping she would ask me to stay with her, I was ready to see what other tricks she had in her arsenal. The movie was pretty good despite the obvious fact that lots of it was not filmed in NYC, let alone Harlem. When the movie ended, I turned my phone back on. About 10 text messages and 4 voicemail messages. **Karen!** My face must have given me away because on cue, Sarah said, "Kristen, what's wrong?" I didn't want this to be a concern, so I said nothing. I don't think she brought it.

"I need to check in with my mom."

"Okay." I called my mother and spoke for five minutes as we walked.

"Just making sure you are okay." I said into the phone.

"Krissy, you were just here." My mom replied.

"Mom, I know but I'm allowed to worry."

She was so sure about everything. "It is going to be fine."

When I hung up, Sarah gently grabbed my hand and this time a sense of calm came with her touch. We went up to her place and after settling inside she asked, "Do you want a glass of wine."

"I would love some."

She poured a glass and handed it to me. I took a sip. "This is tasty. I know I've never had this before, what's it called?

"Golan, it's a Moscato. Are you hungry?"

"Not really, too many snacks."

"I'm going to shower. Feel free to turn on the television and watch what you want."

"Can I join you?" I felt the need to throw caution to the wind. I had never been this comfortable with someone I dated. Plus, I didn't want to think about my mom, work and all my other responsibilities for a while.

Sarah

I could tell something was bothering her however, I didn't want to push the issue. When she was ready to confide in me, I felt she would. The Kristen I knew had no issue in expressing her feelings. When she proposed to take a shower with me, I couldn't believe it, but I wasn't stopping it. I felt last night was a drunken night of ecstasy. When we got in the shower, I offered to wash her back and she agreed.

"I can't let my hair get wet. I don't want to frizz."

I chuckled. “I get it.” I reached my hand out the shower and grabbed a shower cap. I put it on her head to protect her curly mane.”

“Thank you.” She smiled.

I washed her back gently in circles. You could see she was relaxed. She then turned around.

“Want me to wash yours?” I didn’t respond. I lowered my mouth and began sucking on her breast holding the small of her back. She let out a moan telling me she was completely enjoying my sexual advances. I took it further and fingered her gently while I continued kissing her neck and then her lips covered mine. I was giving into passionate kisses under the water. After we washed and toweled off, we made our way to the bedroom. I gave her a t-shirt to slip into and I put on shorts and a t-shirt. I turned on the television and for a while we laid there watching The American. Kristen fell asleep and I let her rest. I got up to do some work at the computer. Apparently, she never turned her phone off. I could hear it buzzing away in her bag.

The next morning, I roused Kristen awake. She looked so peaceful asleep. I lightly kissed her face.

"How did you sleep?" She looked at me as if my question made no sense.

"Too good. I am so comfortable here."

"I'm glad. Are you hungry?" It was a sunny Sunday morning, gorgeous outside. I wanted to give her a little more than I did the night before. Before she answered she started touching the side of my face and kissing me again. Apparently, she wasn't ready to leave the bed. I pulled the t-shirt off and nibbled at her nipples for a while, her moans were soft like a cat purr. I stopped and looked in her eyes and kissed around her vagina. Making her crazy with anticipation. I slowly worked her clit over with my tongue. I held onto her ass getting her in the right position and preventing her from movement so when I gave her enough pressure to make her climax, she could not escape the pleasure. She let out a moderate scream and yelled my name. “Saaarah.” I released her legs and she was still. I broke the silence, "You okay?”

“I am better than okay.”

“Good. You may want to check your phone. It was ringing a lot last night." I started to wonder if there was someone else because the phone calls and text were happening very often. For my own peace of mind and because I was enjoying this weekend and wanted to continue to spend time with Kristen, I had to ask.

"Are you seeing someone else?"

"No, not at all."

"Look, I really enjoy your company and would like to continue to get to know you, but I don't want to pursue you knowing you are involved with someone else."

"Sarah, I'm here with you. This is where I want to be." Hopefully that last statement was the truth.

Kristen

After that conversation, I realized I needed to change my number. I just did not know how to explain to Sarah what had been going on with Karen. I will figure it out when the time comes. My phone had nine texts, six missed calls and three voicemail messages. This was getting crazy. Sarah took me to brunch at Bourbon Street Bar and Grille on Restaurant Row, which isn't so far from her home. During the meal we spoke about music, theater, dance and art. It was nice to be with someone who was into similar things. It prompted me to ask if she would like to go to the Studio Museum in Harlem to see the Romare Bearden exhibit. She was game and after brunch we took the ride up to

Harlem. As we viewed the pieces, we spoke about the feelings they brought up for each of us. We stopped at a piece that was entitled House in Cotton Field! I immediately got teary eyed.

"What made you cry?"

"Being reminded of the hardship we faced and I continue to face every day. It is hard to deal with the fact that you don't fit society's idea of what is beautiful, or that you are second rate because of the melanin in your skin. I'm sure of myself now, but as a teenager, I struggled. Especially as a dancer. Most of my competition was white and I had to work extra hard, at everything." Sarah naturally has a supportive nature. She stood behind me and held me while we stared at the painting for a bit longer. We left the museum and decided to go our separate ways for the night with the promise of reconnecting soon. I walked home from 125th street and realized I needed to check in with my mother. When I called, my aunt answered.

"Hello Krissy."

"Auntie Jan?"

"Yes. How are you?"

"I'm good." My mom and I were close. Auntie Jan was the person I confided in and like my parents she loved me unconditionally. She told me when I was wrong and never held back.

"Auntie, is she sleeping?"

"Yes, she is having a hard day."

"In that case, I won't come by today. I need to finish up some work anyway."

"I want to see you soon. We have a few things to discuss." The seriousness in her voice let me know that my mom was not getting better. I ached.

"Is Thursday good? About eight?"

"Yes, it is. I will see you then and bring wine." My mom was dying. Something I couldn't even fathom. This would soon make me an orphan. I honestly believed my mother's will to live diminished the day my father died. Something changed in her that day; she lost that twinkle in her eye that was once so bright. My parents' thirty years of marriage was an inspiration and I'd hoped to find someone to love of my own.

I reached home to see that I had a blinking light alerting me to messages left. This was ridiculous. All these messages from Karen. I turned on music to choreograph the rest of this dance. By the time I tried several things out, I was tired. I showered and made myself a salad for dinner. I picked up my cell and the moment I did, my phone rang. I immediately thought, *Karen*. I really did not want to be bothered, but it wasn't Karen.

"Hi Sarah." I had a smile on my face.

"I wanted to say goodnight and ask when we could see each other again?"

"This week is pretty busy for me. Can we talk throughout the week and say tentatively Friday?"

"That sounds good to me."

"By the way, would you go to a wedding with me? A friend of mine from college, Clarke is getting married and I'd love it if you would come."

"That sounds intimate."

"Intimate?"

"Yes, I am meeting your friends. Attending a major life event with you."

"I think you are a suitable date."

"Suitable?"

"More than suitable."

"I like the sound of that."

"Sleep well and I will call you tomorrow."

"Good night Sarah."

Thursday with my aunt didn't happen, so I saw her Friday night, which meant that I was unable to see Sarah. She sounded disappointed but, was very understanding. I promised her that we would see one another very soon. Wine in hand, I walked into eggplant Parmesan with Italian bread and a beautiful salad, mixed greens, red and yellow peppers, cherry tomatoes, corn, shredded carrots. It smelled heavenly. My mom and aunt are awesome cooks. They learned the southern recipes at my grandma's side and then explored dishes from other cultures as they grew older. While neither of them went on to do it professionally, so many people have enjoyed delicious meals that they have prepared. While eating dinner we did the small talk for some time starting with my personal life.

"Her name is Sarah and she is a social worker. I was skeptical at first, but she is a good person. I probably will see her tomorrow."

"You look and sound like you are falling for her, Niece."

"I really like her. I don't want to jump in head first. I want to feel it out. You know, but go with the flow." I guess I had this far off look in my eye that was saying more than I wanted to admit. I wasn't purposely rushing anything.

"I hear you saying one thing, however your body language is saying something totally different."

"She wasn't what I expected at all. She definitely is aware of her privilege, she is fun, easy to talk to. I can be my authentic self."

"I like how that sounds." I could tell she was dragging out the good conversation because one of the most difficult we would ever have, was about to happen.

"Auntie, you're making it worse by stalling."

"Krissy, your mom isn't doing so great. It is time to prepare for her final arrangements. We have her life insurance to cover the majority of the costs."

"What cost? I thought she paid for the casket and plot when daddy died."

"She did, I meant other small things like the funeral home costs, flowers. Should we get new dress or use something she already has and just get it dry cleaned?" It really hit me that I was going to have no parents to speak of. I began to cry, tears slowly streaming down my face. No hysterics. My heart felt heavy; I missed my mother already. She hadn't been her vibrant self in a long while. I know when she leaves us here in the natural, I will yearn for her comfort and hugs. I felt like I had lost the very best parts of myself. Being an only child, you are especially special to your parents, because you are the only one.

"Sweetie, it will be okay. I know that losing your mom is hard. I understand that. I also understand that you have to carry the burden alone because you have no siblings, but you have a host of people who love you. Me being first on the list. I cannot be your mother, but I will do my best to be there for as I always have been."

“I know and I love you for it. I just can't believe I am going to be an orphan.”

“It is a hard concept to grasp. Your mother and I went through it. We held on to each other.”

“I am glad the two of you remained close.” Auntie began to tell old stories of when she and my mother were girls. We laughed and it helped me to cheer up and to eat some dessert. The conversation had taken a turn to happier days.

I left my auntie's and walked home to be alone with my thoughts. When I reached my building, I called Sarah, "Sorry we couldn't meet up this evening."

"Me too, but I understood. That is why our plans were tentative."

"What is your day like tomorrow?"

"Nothing much. I know it is lame, but I did my laundry tonight that I had planned to do tomorrow, so I am free."

"I've got some early morning errands and by 2pm, I am all yours."

"Great, see you tomorrow."

Sarah

I was so happy that Kristen was letting me into her life. I could see that some parts were off limits, but I didn't want to push. I've learned that people will give more of themselves in their own time if you allow them to. It is all about building trust. I felt good about where this was going and wanted to enjoy the ride. Besides she wasn't the only one who didn't want to be completely open about their life. My parents were by far, not the best. My father drank and my mother just did what he said. My mother worked, but it was never consistent or long term.

The week went by with phone calls and text, but not physical contact. I missed her scent it was fading too quickly. It was a Friday night and we spoke about making plans for the next day. I could barely sleep because of all the excitement and anticipation. We met at 59th and Columbus and got a late lunch at Whole Foods.

"I had no idea they had snack packs in Whole Foods." I said as we were looking to find a spot to sit and eat.

"They are my favorite. Sometimes, I buy a roll or bagel and put the chicken salad on it. The thing is though, you have to add mustard and then it is perfect."

"So basically, it isn't good until you add the mustard?"

"I wouldn't say that. The mustard just gives it more flavor."

"Right, bland white people chicken salad, until a little love of flavor."

"Something like that." We laughed. I loved that she didn't cringe at my assessment and just went with the conversation. It wasn't an awkward interaction.

I loved her Saturday ensemble. I was admiring it since we met up. She wore a cute brown skirt and blue top, knee high brown boots, with a flower adorning her curly hair. We sat down in a remote part of the park with little to no traffic and began to eat.

"Well, let's see how this chicken salad measures up." I took spoonful and tasted it.

"Not bad, I give it a solid eight."

"An eight? Really? Why is that?" She was offended.

"It is really tasty, but something is still missing."

"Even with the mustard."

I added a little salt. Stirred it a bit. Then I tasted it. "Whoa. Now this is amazing."

"Salt huh?"

"I probably eat too many salty things, but this is good.

"See, told you." She said as we continued eating our lunch.

When we were done, I asked. "Where do you usually have dessert?"

"A few places. Levain, the chocolate walnut cookies are great. They are by me on 8th and 117th. Although there is another location on Amsterdam, I think by like 73rd street. I also love the banana pudding at Magnolia Bakery. I would say those are my favorites for now. Wait! One more. When it is late, Insomnia Cookies."

"I know all about them. I like to take the oatmeal raisin and make an ice cream sandwich."

"I have never done that before. I'd be willing to try."

As we talked, I put my hand on her knee enjoying the conversation. After a silence, Kristen put her hand on top of mine and guided it up her skirt. Her tights were crotchless. I was in for a treat. I traced my finger outside her lips, until I got to her vagina, flicking my finger in and out. She giggled and slightly moaned with her eyes locked on mine, daring me to go further. When I pulled my finger out, I tasted her warm juices from my finger.

"Can we go back to your place?"

"Sure, if that is what you want."

"Yes, I do." We took the shortest cab ride to my apartment. I sat her up on top of the island, once we got in. Leaving her clothes on, I sucked on her clitoris like life depended on it. Fingering her for emphasis. I strapped on turned her ass in the air and invaded her vagina with the dildo. She took in all of it. I knew this piece was perfect when I brought it last night. I pumped and pumped until she said no more. She got down off the island and went to the bedroom. I followed her and watched her lay on her back. She then asked, "Put it in my ass?" I was a little shocked, I didn't want to make the moment uncomfortable and I was feeling unnerved.

"Kris, you've done this before?"

"Once, but it was an awful experience. I trust you and feel like you will be gentle."

"I'm going to get some lube." I went in the bathroom and returned with the lube. I slowly slid the dildo in and soon began to pump in and out. Periodically asking if she was okay. Her phone kept ringing. We stopped. I went in the bathroom to clean up and she followed. Holding me while I stood in the mirror. I turned and started kissing her lightly. Tears came to her face. She was hurting. I was hesitant to ask why, but I felt protective of her and her feelings. I really liked her.

"Kris, why are you crying?" She attempted to speak, but no words came. I took her by the hand and we sat on the couch. I just held her while she sobbed. Finally, the tears stopped.

"I'm sorry about that. It is just, I guess I am always holding it together and it, I feel safe with you. I needed to release."

"What's on your mind?"

"You know my father passed a few years ago." I gave her a nod to signify that I remembered.

"Well my mom is soon to follow and I'm having a hard time accepting it."

"That is completely understandable. Did you see a therapist after your dad passed?"

"No, why?"

"Sometimes it helps for people to talk about their loss while grieving. Because you may be experiencing this again, you may want to consider it."

"Let me think about it. How come you never talk about your family?"

"Not much to say."

"What are your parents like?"

"Honestly, they are not good people. When I got old enough, I spent more time at Jeff's house. I felt safe there. His parents were kind people." Even saying that much took me back to some parts of my life I would rather forget.

To get out of the somber mood I created, I suggested we go to Pig & Whistle. When we got there, it was a nice crowd of people. We went to the bar and ordered drinks. When I finished my drink, I got up and started dancing. Kris was surprised this white girl has moves. She then got up and joined me.

"I so love that you can dance. It is fun to be with someone who enjoys it as much as me."

"I haven't done that in a long time. We should go again soon."

"We will. At the wedding. You are still coming, right?" How could I resist that smile? She was gorgeous and I wanted to be more than her date. I was striving to be her partner.

"Of course." We sat to take a breath at the bar and ordered some bar food and a second round of drinks, before it could arrive, a song I didn't know came on and Kristen was back on the dance floor. I loved her energy. While she danced, my phone buzzed. I looked at the screen. A text from Jeff. *Hey, what's up with you? Haven't heard from you. Hit me up and get your face out of the new pussy. LOL.* I grinned at the screen. Then responded. *You have no sense. I am good. We are out dancing. Hit you back soon.* I looked up from my phone and Kristen was still grooving to the beats streaming through the speakers. While we didn't dance all night, we definitely were there for about four hours. We made our way back to my place after and crashed.

Kristen

Two weeks went by quickly and in that time, I had enjoyed my time with Sarah, completed the dances for my junior high kids and watched my mom deteriorate. My mom was now in a rehabilitation facility and Aunt Jan and I had discussed clearing out her apartment. She wasn't going to return home.

The night before the wedding, Sarah stayed with me for the first time. It was nice having her in my space, but I know that she noticed the frequent phone calls. I ended up turning the ringer off. "Kristen, you are the only one I know who still has a landline."

"My mother insisted when I moved in and I never got rid of it. I often have the calls forwarded to my cell because very few people have the number. "

"That makes sense."

I cooked for her for the first time too. Macaroni and cheese, fried chicken and greens with corn bread. Her eyes were big when we sat at my small dining room table. "Who did you make all this food for?"

"I made it for us."

"It looks like too much."

"I made enough to have leftovers."

"Oh, I see."

After dinner, we laid in bed and watched whatever was on. We ended up turning in pretty early, knowing we had quite the day ahead.

The next morning the sun was bright and woke me up at 6am. I just laid there staring at the ceiling thinking about all that was going on in my life and while some of it sad, I turned to see the bright spot that had entered my life, Sarah. We had a small breakfast, showered, dressed, put make up and were out the door. The Uber arrived as we walked out the building door and off to the church we went for the wedding. Sarah was wearing a cream linen suit that was perfect. I had on my bridesmaid dress, a high low dress with a sheer mesh top and felt quite sassy. My hair had grown long enough to have straw curls.

We arrived and went straight into the bathroom closest to the bridal suite. Sarah was staring at me as I put the finishing touches on my makeup. "You look beautiful."

"Why, thank you? You're looking pretty hot yourself."

"Why, thank you." We giggled! We walked into the bridal suite and I see my girl and she is stunning. Clarke had a beautiful beaded mermaid dress on, neutral makeup with this lip color that was popping off of the subtle canvas of her face. I introduced Sarah to Clarke and Kasey. Sarah kissed me and left the bridal suite to sit with guests.

The radiant bride waited for the door to close and said, "She is very cute."

"Forget that, what's the sex like?" Kasey jumped in.

"Gosh Kasey get out the girl's business. So, how is the sex?" We all cracked up.

"Let us just say, no complaints. How are things working for you and your almost husband?" I asked.

"Singing, *Iiii can't get enough of yo love babe."* The room erupted with laughter. Always fun times when the three of us get together. Kasey wanted to share her fun times too.

"Don't leave me out. Gave him some while driving." Kasey always lived dangerously when it came to sex.

"You did not!" Clarke yelped.

"Oh yes. He forced me to stop before an accident happened."

"Girl, you are crazy." I could not believe she was engaging in this immature undergraduate behavior.

This reunion banter happened for about five more minutes and then... We immediately stopped the conversation as Clarke's mom walked in barking orders. We all had residual smirks. Clarke glowed and her smile was saying how delighted she was to walk down the aisle and meet her future husband. The ceremony was very short and Clarke's cousins sang Ribbon in the Sky with violin accompaniment. It was different, yet magnificent. Their sound was incomparable, I had never heard anything like it. I liked it so much my emotions got the better of me. I cried just a tad, but I wasn't alone. Sarah gave me reassuring smiles throughout the ceremony.

When we finally got to our seats at the reception, Sarah whispered, "I love you." I was taken aback, but more so because I had responded in kind. It was just a little over a month of dating. Instead of consuming myself with all the what ifs, I enjoyed the moment and savored it. This was the way I felt things should be when you meet someone. An organic coming together and not feeling forced to share your time or uncomfortable, but coming together with ease and cohesion.

Kasey and I were standing at the bar refreshing our drinks and I was waiting for her to ask and no sooner than I finished ordering mine and Sarah's drink, she asked, "Did you do what I told you to do?"

"Not yet."

"What are you waiting for?" She asked with a sour face.

Then the blushing bride walks over, "What are you two discussing?" I shot Kasey a look like don't you dare bring this up with her on her wedding day.

"Oh nothing, just teasing Krissy about having a white girl that can dance."

"You two do look good out there." Clarke grinned. Then she was summoned away.

"If you don't get that Order of Protection as soon as possible. Ugh. I don't want her to do anything stupid."

"I know. I hear you. Sis, I promise I will take care of it. I am going to get back to dancing. Besides, don't you have someone waiting to keep you occupied?" Her new beau was steadily glancing in our direction. Plus, I didn't want to continue the conversation about order of protections and creepy Karen. It turned my stomach just thinking about the entire deal. Sarah and I danced and danced. I got a few more moments with my girls, some great pictures for memories, and cake to take home. We, Kasey, Clarke and I promised to spend time together once Clarke got back from her honeymoon. The day was magical.

Sarah

Kristen was still holding back something. I could feel the tension every time one of her phones rang. The calls were getting to be annoying, aggravating and troublesome. I continued to let things go in a natural course. One Saturday, Kristen asked me to meet her aunt. I was nervous because Kris had described her as a sharp shooter of sorts. I was nervous. I showed up to Kris' house right on time. I brought her flowers and two bottles of wine.

Kris made a light pasta dish with shrimp and vegetables. Her aunt got started early, *where did you grow up, what do your parents do, how did Kris and I meet?* Felt like I was on an interview. I didn't feel uncomfortable though.

"I grew up upstate and I don't have much of a relationship with my parents. Kris and I met at a coalition meeting. She tells me you are in social services." I felt I should show my interest and that would balance all of the questions.

"Yes, I run a group home on the Lower East Side."

"Really. Is it co-ed?"

"No, just boys."

"You're the first woman I've met that runs a group home. There are very few group homes in existence these days."

"Right, the ones left are for the hard to place children. Believe me it is no easy task. I am a woman, African American and educated."

"I think that is awesome. I hope to be able to run a program one day. Is it okay if I visit at some point?" Kris smiled. I could tell that this conversation had won her aunt's approval.

"Of course, I would love to show you around a bit and talk about the systems at play. I hope to retire soon and just consult. That will give me a little more freedom." We had dessert that Aunt Jan made, bread pudding, her staple I was told, good and sweet. It was perfect.

Aunt Jan said, "The key is to use a bread that will stand up to the egg mixture." There was a sauce she poured on top made with bourbon that was delectable. We finished both bottles of wine and Aunt Jan announced that she was leaving. We said goodnight and sat talking for what felt like an eternity. Until we fell asleep on the couch. I woke up at 3am and got Kris up to get in bed. Sunday at 10am, her phone rang incessantly. She answered half awake, half asleep. "Hello." Whoever was on the line made her alert and she got up. "Stop calling me. I want no part of you." She sounded angry.

"Kris, what's going on?"

"My ex keeps calling and harassing me."

"How long has this been going on?"

"For months."

"Why haven't you said anything?"

"I didn't want this to be your problem."

"If we are going to be together, we have to be honest."

"I hear that, but his isn't your problem."

"First things first, change your cell number and then you need to go to the precinct and get an order of protection."

"Too many people have the number. I can't change it."

"At least block her."

"I have, but then she uses different numbers to call from."

"In that case, you may have to change the number."

"I have been meaning to go to the precinct, but there is never enough time. I will do those things this week."

For the first time since we got together, I saw a very different side of Sarah.

More aggressive and take charge. Somehow, she convinced me that we should do a self-defense class. So now, once a week we are at the Harlem Y doing self-defense classes. Initially, I thought this was pointless, but quickly realized it was a nice way to deal with stress and tension.

Sarah had a late client and I went to class alone. I left the "Y" and who do I run into on the corner of 7th Avenue and 135th street? Karen.

"Where are you coming from?" Karen was undressing me with her eyes and making me uncomfortable. My skin was crawling.

"That is not your concern."

"Really now? I guess you changing your number isn't my concern either."

"Exactly." I made a mad dash across the street and for once the M2 was right on time. I got on that bus and attempted to calm down. I hoped I wouldn't run into her again, but I'm sure she pieced together that I was coming from the "Y" considering I had my workout clothes on. I was rattled and called Sarah.

"Hey, what's up?" She answered in a jovial voice.

"I ran into Karen."

Her voice went from upbeat to one of concern. "You sound upset, what happened?"

"Nothing really, I... I just don't want to be alone."

"Keep calm, go to my house. I will be there as soon as I can." I felt privileged that I had keys to Sarah's house. She said it made things easy considering I was spending lots of time there. Actually, my clothes were also moving in too. I was at ease with Sarah, it felt natural. When she got in, she sat her things down and hugged me tightly.

"That hug felt good. I needed that. Thank you."

"How are you feeling though?"

"I am still a little weirded out that I ran into her. I was coming out of the Y, my mind on other things and there she was."

"I can't imagine how you feel. It must have been awkwardly surprising and off putting."

"That is an understatement. I just don't want Aunt Jan to know. She has enough to deal with. My mom is not getting better, although she is holding on."

After a grand dinner of creamy salmon with Dijon sauce and a side of asparagus with Bartenura Sparkling Moscato Rose she made love to me like never before. It was dessert with dessert. Sarah made me sticky with chocolate and caramel and dipped strawberries in it. She fed them to me as her Jazz Soul playlist filled the room. That was one of those nights that you hoped would never end.

The next morning, I woke up in tears. I was screaming and Sarah was lightly shaking me awake.

"Kris, wake up, your dreaming."

"Huh. What?"

"Babe, you're dreaming. You're okay."

"Oh my God. It felt. It felt so real. I was running and running. I was being chased by Karen. She was gaining on me."

"It is over." She held me after the nightmare. I fell back to sleep. We woke again from the ringing of my phone.

"Hello. Hey girl, you still sleep?" It was Kasey.

"Tough night."

"You are still coming later, right?"

"I wouldn't miss it."

Sarah came out of the bathroom. "Everything okay?"

"Yes," I said while I put on my shirt. "I am going out with the girls tonight."

"I think that would be good for you. You coming back here tonight?"

"Only if you want me too."

"Of course, I do."

We kissed and I didn't want to go, but work called.

Surprisingly my day went well. Sarah texted me a few times in between sessions. I loved that she was letting me know she was thinking of me when we weren't together. I was happy to have leftovers for my lunch. My students seemed to catch the concepts that I was teaching for the day. I stayed late at school doing lesson plans and tidying up my classroom. It was a productive way to kill time before meeting up with Clarke and Kasey. Then off to happy hour at Verlaine. We ordered appetizers, sangria and lychee martinis.

"How was the trip, Clarke?" I said as the drinks came to the table.

"It was so good." She took out her phone to show pictures. "Honestly it was hard to come home to the reality of work and bills, well life. Adulting is so hard."

Kasey took a sip of her drink and got up to go to the bathroom with her mouth covered by her hands like she was about to vomit everywhere. "Clarke, what's that about?"

"Well, either she is sick or pregnant."

"You think pregnant?"

"When does Kasey get sick from alcohol. Except..."I

"Except that time I visited y'all at school when we all played that drinking game and were completely wasted." We busted out laughing.

"That was messy."

"I don't think I want to ever be drunk like that again."

Kasey came back over to the table. Clarke and I just looked at her.

"What? Why are you both looking at me like I have a loch ness monster on my head?"

"Have you taken a test?" Clarke asked.

"A test for what?"

"Girl, don't play." I chimed in. "A pregnancy test."

"For what?" Kasey says in her naivety.

"Really?!" We got the check and took our appetizers to go. We walked over to the Duane Reade and brought a three pack.

"I can't possibly be pregnant."

"Well, we are just going to have to get confirmation and go from there." Clarke said as a matter of fact. Instead of taking the train up, we took an Uber. We walked into Kasey's sunken-in apartment. While she went in the bathroom, Clarke and I poured ourselves something to drink. When she came out the bathroom, she had a face that could not be read. Law school game face is what we called it. So, I teased a bit. "The verdict is?"

"It is positive."

Clarke and I gushed. "Awww, Kasey is going to be a momma." We were so happy, but Kasey did not appear to be.

"Girl, what is the matter? This is a blessing." Clarke said.

"Justin and I got into a fight after we went to my parents' house and I haven't spoken to him since." We both gave Kasey a blank stare and Clarke says, "Sis, that was weeks ago. You have to call him and let him know what's going on. He deserves to know."

"I will. I just can't believe this is happening."

"Clarke and I have your back and you can provide a good life for this baby."

"I am glad I have you two. Not only do I have to deal with Justin but, my mother. She probably will have some very unsavory things to say." Kasey said.

"Maybe, but eventually she will have to get over it." Clarke said.

"Just make sure you call the doctor in the morning and make an appointment." I wanted to make sure that she got a blood test even though the home pregnancy test gave a positive result. Clarke and I left to go home. Kasey was tired and look like she needed some rest.

I got back to Sarah's about 9:30pm or so. It was good to see my girls and one of us was about to become a mother. How exciting?
I walked in and Sarah was watching a movie on tv. She pressed pause and I realized she was catching up on a show via Hulu. She asked. "How was it?"

"Great, Kasey's having a baby. I didn't think she would be first."

"Life happens. You never know which way things will turn out."

"I know, happy for her and hope she works things out with Justin."

"What's up with that?"

"They got into an argument and haven't been speaking."

"Oh."

"Exactly. We told her to call him and the doctor to make an appointment. He has a right to know about the baby. She seemed a little scared."

"I think that is all normal considering it doesn't sound as if they were planning to get pregnant. How are you doing?

"It was a good day. I got a lot accomplished and tomorrow I will teach the girls the finale after school."

"You finished it."

"Yes, I am excited about it."

"As you should be." It was nice to have Sarah support my work. It was nice to feel someone else's excitement about something I was doing. That night I went to sleep feeling a level of peace I hadn't felt in some time.

Sarah

Happy she was back at my house. As we got ready for bed, I made sure to ask her if she was feeling better about Karen. She said she was okay, but I wasn't so sure. I waited for her to drift to sleep first. She appeared so peaceful. I allowed myself to finally stop fighting sleep myself.

I opened my eyes and looked at the alarm clock. It was late. Was I seeing correctly, 3:30am? Ugh who is calling her phone at this hour. I knew it couldn't be Karen because she didn't have the new number. I didn't answer Kristen's phone ever. It stopped and then mine began to ring. The hair on my neck began to rise. I felt something was wrong.

"Hello, Aunt Jan."

"Sarah, where's Krissy?"

"She's sleeping. Is everything okay?"

"No honey, you have to wake her. Her mother's gone."

"Where should we meet you?"

"Come to the rehab." I was not ready for this at all. I've lost family of my own, but this was Kristen's mother. I know nothing about the loss of a parent and even if one of them passed away, I don't know what I would feel. They had problems and finding out I was a lesbian fueled the fire. A few weeks ago, Kris's mom took a turn for the worse and was put in a rehabilitation center in hopes she would improve. She was sad about her mother being there, but another fall could not be risked. I silently asked the universe for strength to be a good support.

"Kris, wake up." I tried to rouse her, but it wasn't easy.

"Kris, baby, you gotta get up."

"Why, it isn't morning? The sun is not up."

"Aunt Jan called." I couldn't get the rest out. She must have known. She cried and screamed no for about five minutes. I held her. Her spirit was broken. Her Soul was hurting. She was Emotionally wrecked. Knowing her mother had left earth must have felt like her world was ending too. I'm not particularly spiritual. I hoped her mother had found her husband again, all of her ancestors and was at peace. I prayed for the first time in such a long time. I used to go to church sometimes with Jeff and his family. I liked it, but I didn't feel like I was one of God's chosen because of my home life. My parents told me I would go to hell for my sexual orientation. I thought God loved everyone. At least that seemed to be the central message of Pastor Floyd's sermons. I prayed for Kris and Aunt Jan. We dressed and went to the nursing home. The cab ride was quick with traffic being almost nonexistent. She cried and cried and when we arrived it took a few minutes for her to go inside. Aunt Jan met us and she hugged Kris and told her all the things she needed to hear.

She held my hand tightly as we went to see her mother. She cried and when it felt that all her tears were spent, she cried some more. There was paperwork to complete and arrangements to make. By the time we left the nursing home it was about 7am. We were all tired and needed to make arrangements for work. It was a Friday and I felt no guilt in not going in. The next few days proved to be very difficult. I helped as much as I could and felt very appreciated. I just wish I had not met her extended family under these circumstances.

The funeral was the most uplifting I had ever attended. I honestly didn't feel sad. I was glad Kris' mom wasn't in pain anymore. The night of the funeral, Kris was very horny. While at Aunt Jan's she pulled me into the bathroom. It was crazy, but I felt like a teenager again. Slightly invigorated. When we got back to her apartment, she was all over me. I responded in kind. She needed to be loved and I understood that. I tasted her all over the house. We lay in bed talking about her mother and things she remembered about her parents during childhood.

"One time, we went to the beach, just us three. My mom packed sandwiches, fruits, snacks and drinks. I remember us burying my dad in the sand. Only his head and toes were exposed. It was so funny." Her reminiscing seemed to be helpful. There were moments when she cried and laughed and moments when both were happening. Unlike me, Kristen shared a very loving story about her coming out. It seemed that we never stop coming out. For most young people, your parents are the hardest. Especially if you are living in their home at the time. Apparently, Kristen's parents knew and told her it was okay because they would love her no matter what. Much like the way Jeff's family treated me.

Kristen

I woke up with a tear stained pillow. It was a Wednesday and Sarah had gone to work. I was happy all of my extended family and friends were supporting me through this rough time in my life. Sometimes getting out of bed was hard. Sometimes, I couldn't stop crying. Sometimes, I was angry at God. Mostly, I wanted to be laying in between my parents. Today, I felt good. I showered, dressed and went for a walk around Sarah's neighborhood. I ended up walking north and west by Lincoln Center, sat by the water and lost track of time, just relaxing. Ended up there three hours before I realized how long I had been sitting. I picked myself up and went home. I picked up my gym bag and went to the "Harlem Y". Spent a half hour doing laps in the pool. Rode the bike for a half hour and felt done. I wanted to go to Aunt Jan's for a bit. As I exited, there she was... Karen! My reaction was to walk the other way, but she grabbed me by my shirt, "Not so fast. Where do you think you are going?" I didn't respond. Her grip was tight on my arm. She had been working out, her muscles were defined. She wore black shorts, black tank top, boots, all of her femininity gone. It was her work clothes, minus the hard hat.

"Let's walk and don't make a scene." She made me walk to St. Nicholas Park. More like marched me to the park. Her grip on my arm was tight. Her nails pierced my skin. She stripped me down to my bra and panties, as she spewed obscenities. Called me a bitch, a whore, told me I wasn't shit for being with a white woman. She had been spying on Sarah and I. Then my underwear was torn away. Her body hovering over me, creating a shadow. I could not see the sun. I struggled to get up, but she punched me in the eye. As the tears streamed my face, praying for help, she said, "Shut your fucking mouth. You better not attempt to call for help or I will punch you in the fucking face again." To ensure I wouldn't she took the bandana from her neck and shoved it in my mouth. The taste was awful sweaty cotton.

I was so scared, my heart was racing, my tears were coming faster. I kicked and flailed until I was tired. She took a branch, spread my legs with her elbow. She hit my legs so they would stop moving. The branch broke on the last strike. She retrieved a second branch from a nearby tree. She examined it. I had so many things running through my mind. I was praying to God that I would be saved. Someone would find me. She continued to examine her find that was thicker with several bumps where buds would form. Then she said, "this will do" and with no remorse and hatred in her eyes, shoved it in my vagina with a force that made my insides hurt. I attempted to twist my body away.

"You better stop struggling." She yelled. Then she pulled the branch out and hit me again. The pain was unthinkable. I felt like my insides were being grated and shredded. My right eye was nearly shut. She kept shoving that branch in me, over and over with brute force. The erroneous pain made me black out. I don't remember what happened after. When I came to, there was an officer standing over me. I attempted to struggle with him, but blacked out again.

My head hurt so bad. The next time I came to, I was in the hospital. I felt my eye stinging and my lip felt swollen. I heard voices. None I recognized. They were saying things like, she fought hard. It was a hate crime, they said. She got skin cells under her nails. She will survive, but she may not have children. The more and more lucid I became, the more the pain was prevalent. I was hurt. My throat was dry. My tongue cracked.

"Water, I need water." I saw someone checking things. She didn't hear me. I barely heard me. I tried again.

"Water, may I have water?"

"Hello there. How are you feeling? I will give you water." She poured the water and I drank it down through the straw.

"May I have more please" She poured more into the cup. "How long have I been here?"

"Two days. Can we call someone for you?"

"Yes, my aunt and my girlfriend." I wrote the numbers down and the nurse left to call. I couldn't imagine why no one called them sooner. Maybe my stuff was stolen by Karen. A plain clothes officer came to talk to me. Asked me a multitude of questions. It was very confusing. My memory felt hazy. Auntie Jan had showed up and was furious at the situation. I am glad she got there first.

"How do you feel?"

"Awful. I'm physically in pain. I can't believe this happened. Why would she do this to me. All because she felt rejected. I am afraid to see Sarah. What will she think of me now? The doctor said there was a lot of internal damage and I may not be able to have children. I never thought about whether I wanted to or not, but now the choice has been taken away."

"Krissy, please calm yourself. Sarah loves you. Don't worry about that right now. You have to heal. As far as having children, you will figure out what you want to do when the time comes." I sobbed and mourned the loss of what had been taken away from me with Karen's brutal attack. Auntie Jan and I continued to talk and then, finally, she showed up.

Sarah

I was not prepared to see the woman I love, mangled. Her lips dry and cracked, her face bruised, hands scarred from fighting back. It hurt to see her that way, but I held the tears. I wanted to show her I was strong. As difficult as it was, I held my own.

"Oh my God. I can't believe she did this to you. How do you feel?" I said, trying not to look too shocked and amazed.

"I am very sore. Moderate pain. My throat is starting to feel better. Auntie, can you give us a minute to talk?"

"Sure honey, I am going to give Clarke and Kasey a call."

"Thank you Auntie."

When she asked Aunt Jan to leave us alone for a minute, that put me on edge. What did she need to say that her aunt could not hear? Aunt Jan reluctantly left the room.

"Sarah, I don't want you to see me like this. I think we should… or should-."

"Should what? Break up? I am with you because I love you and I want to be."

"I know, but I am going through so much right now. I need to sort it all out."

"You can't do that with me in your life?"

"I just think it is best for me to work this out on my own."

"Do you really want me to go?" Her silence was loud. Her tears made it clear. I was so hurt; I didn't know what to do. How could she?

"Just until things return to normal." Returned to normal. I refused to cry. Refused to give her the satisfaction. Does she not realize? Nothing will ever be the same. I left the room, no retort, no goodbye. Just movement out of her space. Aunt Jan was out in the hall, speaking to a doctor. I waited until they were done.

"You are a wonderful woman and I'm glad I got to meet you. Take care."

"Sarah, what's going on? Where are you going?"

"She broke up with me." I headed for the elevator and the tears streamed down my face. I felt assaulted by her words and disregard for what we had been building together. I was with her during the loss of her mother. How could she just say that we were over? I felt nauseous I was so angry. I somehow thought she would come live with me after this. I was wrong. That night I went over in my head the past few weeks, our last conversation playing in my head. The next day dragged. I was angry at how she cast me aside and didn't think twice. It hurt when people asked about her. I pray for her daily, to recover and to heal.

A week or so later, I sat home relaxing with music and wine. My phone rang. It was about 10pm, who could be calling at this hour was my first question and when I looked at my phone, I thought, *why is she calling?* My initial reaction was let the voicemail get it. Then I thought to myself she wouldn't be calling if it wasn't important. By the time I decided to answer... it stopped ringing. The voicemail was simple and to the point. *Sarah, it is Auntie. Just checking in on you. Love you.* She was a wonderful woman. It didn't matter if her niece had left me in the lurch, she cared for me and I knew that the relationship we shared was between us. Still it was too soon to be that close to someone that was so close to Kristen. I ached. None of my family lived in New York. I had created a family here. I barely communicate with any of my biological family. Only my cousins, Jennifer and Abigail. Of course, I still had Jeff and his family, but they were not in close proximity. I hadn't talk to him in a few, so I gave him a call.

"Well look who came up for air."

"Damn Jeff, don't be like that."

"Nah, how you?"

"I've been better. Kristen was assaulted badly by her ex-girlfriend."

"Oh shit. She okay?"

"Nah, she has lots of recovering to do and she broke up with me."

"Really?"

"I don't get it."

"Girl, you know she has gone through so much. She needs help."

"Yeah. Apparently, I am not worthy to be there with her through it."

"She may feel like she is a burden or maybe she doesn't want you to see her like that. Didn't you say she was hurt pretty bad."

"Yeah. This is just pissing me off. When are you going to come for a visit?"

"When you coming down?"

"Touché. Let's make it happen. I miss you."

"I know. Later girl." I sat stewing about my relationship ending. I was deeply hurt.

Kristen

The external healing was almost completed. Slight bruising still remained on my cheekbone. However, the emotional and mental pain had gaping holes that did not seem to be getting filled. My mother was gone and was not there to provide emotional support. My most intimate and sacred space had been violated beyond repair. I had returned to work and was glad to have other things to focus on, other than my own hurt. It was very difficult to come up with answers for my students when they asked, where I had been. I had loads of school work to complete as well as end of school planning. My junior high after school dancers were ecstatic when I returned. I worked them hard, but they rose to the challenge. Mostly I plowed through the everyday details, suppressing the emotions that plagued me. The adults at work tiptoed around me, except my good friend Sheena. She stopped by my classroom, "Hey girl, how you doing?"

"I am hanging in there, but everyone is being so weird around me. The students made me feel normal."

"I can imagine that people just don't know what to say. It was on NY1."

"Sheena, I get that, but I just want to go back to being me. Wait, NY1 really?"

"They didn't say a name, but people put it together. It will take time for you to get back to some resemblance of what was. Have you considered that you will have a new normal?

"No, but I guess you are right. Things are different now."

"Have you thought about therapy?"

"I have thought about it, but I haven't called anyone for an appointment."

"When you can, go see Ms. Barth. She has a list of potential therapists. It is good to have social workers on staff. They aren't just here for the students, but the staff too."

"Thanks. I appreciate the conversation. I will go talk to her before the day ends."

I made sure to see Ms. Barth before I left. She gave me four names of people I could potentially see. I knew I needed to talk to someone, so I would not explode or implode for that matter. The nightmares were getting to be too much. I would wake up screaming or sweating from dreams of Karen, stabbing me, chasing me, mutilating me. They were awful. In those moments, Sarah came to mind.

I broke my lease and moved in with Auntie Jan, which was helpful. My landlord was very kind and didn't make me pay the penalty since it was so close to my lease renewal. I helped Clarke and Justin plan the baby shower. It helped to take my mind off of the assault. I was so happy that life was feeling "normal" again. Some things would never be the same. I missed my mother and I missed Sarah. The next week was a coalition picnic. I hoped she would be there. The day of the picnic, I got there early to help set up. The DJ was out playing some great old school music. You know folk can't get together without line dancing. I was walking around and making sure people were enjoying themselves. Of course, I was looking to see if Sarah had come but, she wasn't there. While the day went well, I was disappointed that she had not come.

I got home and thought to call, but didn't. I didn't know how to fix it or even if I could.

Holding in all my emotions wasn't helping. Aunt Jan suggested I make some calls and decide on a therapist. "Sweetie, you need to talk to a professional."

"I have the numbers of a few people that my colleague recommended to me. I just don't know what to say? It is all so overwhelming."

"That is a good place to start."

"I thought I would be over it by now, but I feel so broken."

"You lost your mother and were assaulted in a short span of time. You were physically and emotionally violated. That will take time to work through. It is great that you are trying to get back into the swing of things, but it won't make it go away. You have to face it."

"I hear you Auntie." Thoughts about going to therapy was constantly on my mind. I am not sure what the block was for me. I just could never follow through on calling any of the numbers I had. If I was going to move forward, I would have to do it.

The next day, I called two persons I had on the list. The first was Jennifer Dylan, LCSW and Barbara Hill, LCSW-R. I had only enough energy for those two calls. I left messages for both ladies, but Ms. Hill got back to me. I liked her professionalism. My appointment was scheduled for Saturday morning at 10:15am. I was very nervous and had no idea what to expect. She sent me an intake form via email and a goal form as well. I liked some of the questions that were on the goal form. Imagine you were asleep and woke up with all your problems solved. What things would be changed?

The day of my appointment, I was nervous. Not knowing what to exactly expect, I had my cup of chamomile tea with me to calm my nerves. Ms. Hill began by asking various questions. Some open ended, others very specific. The office was not what I expected. Warm colors covered the walls. Art work reminding me of Gordon Parks photos in Life Magazine adorned the walls. Black and white photos are always so striking to me because it forces you to zone in on the emotions or actions of the persons. There was a desk off to one corner with a chair. The typical couch. Something I didn't expect, a rocker. I love rocking chairs. They are soothing. After formal documents were completed, she jumped right into it.

"What brings you here today?"

"Well, I guess it is because most recently, I've had lots of things happen."

"Please elaborate."

"My mother passed away recently."

"I'm sorry to hear. How has that been for you?"

"It was very overwhelming, but my aunt has been there for me. There was lots of paperwork and things to tend to."

"And your father? Is he part of your life?" That was when I began to well up with tears. I cried for what felt like an eternity. I had no parents; no children and I asked a woman who loved me to not be part of my life anymore.

"My father passed before my mother."

"What are you feeling right now?"

"I feel... alone. abandoned. sad."

"Have you had any thoughts of hurting yourself?"

"No."

"How are you sleeping?"

"Some nights good and others, restless, sometimes nightmares, dreams."

"Tell me about a nightmare and a dream." Where was she going with this line of questioning? Why would this be relevant to what was going on in my life?

"When I dream it is usually about my parents. The nightmares are usually a replay of the incident that happened with my ex with slight variations."

"The incident between you and your ex? Care to elaborate."

"I would prefer not to. I'm not ready to talk about it."

"Besides your aunt, what other supports do you have?"

"My friends, Clarke, Kasey and Sheena."

"Is there a significant other?"

"No, that ended."

"Would you care to elaborate?"

"I ended the relationship because I was afraid."

"Why was that?"

"I felt I was burdening her with my problems." She was pressing on nerves bringing up Sarah and making me think about that shit with Karen. I was told there was enough evidence that I didn't need to testify; however, things could change and I had no desire to face Karen again. I didn't want to face Sarah either.

"I see your body language has changed. What are you feeling right now?"

"I'm angry. I don't want to talk about my ex."

"I'm going to suggest that you continue to do things that make you feel good. Increase your endorphins. Exercise. Eat well. Sleep well. I'd like to see you again next Sat." I left the office ready to do something fun. Like go dancing. I ended up going to swim at another YMCA. I couldn't go back to the Harlem location. I avoided that immediate neighborhood because it was emotionally overwhelming for me. I did laps for about a half hour. The water washing over me felt so good and when I got out, I was hungry and ready to get in bed.

***

My junior high girls were all excited about their show. They looked gorgeous. They had a full performance for the last three days. It was Saturday and the last performance; Aunt Jan planned to attend. During the fifteen-minute intermission, I peeked out at the crowd to see where she was and my eyes could not believe, Sarah was next to her. In full confusion, I was excited, fearful, elated and my anxiety was taking over. I took a few deep breaths.

The girls did such an awesome job for the final performance. They surprised me with flowers and my self-proclaimed leader of the group, Liah, gave a touching speech. Now that the performance was done, I had to face her. With sweaty palms, I walked over toward Sarah and Auntie.

"Hey Auntie, what did you think?"

"They were amazing and that Liah is going places." Auntie Jan replied.

I didn't want to be rude and not speak to her. "Sarah, thanks for coming."

"It was my pleasure. I enjoyed the show. Especially the hip-hop medley."

"I'm going to finish cleaning up. Auntie, I will see you at home. Sarah, thanks again for supporting the show." I didn't know what else to say to her. It was great to see her. The opportunity presented itself to have a conversation and I let it slip away. Make amends, Ms. Hill said. Be honest, Ms. Hill said. There are only two ways it could go, Ms. Hill said. Here was a perfect opportunity and I let it go. I got home and Auntie Jan was watching television.

"Hey Auntie."

"Want some tea?"

"No thanks, I am going to shower and get in bed. I am pretty tired."

The shower washed over me. The scent of my lavender body wash filled the bathroom. I soaped my wash cloth and my body. The hot water rinsing the suds way. I grabbed a comfy night gown and lay in bed staring at the ceiling. Since being brutally mutilated. I hadn't touched myself, except in the shower. I hadn't been touched because I pushed away the woman who would be affectionate, shower me with her love. I hadn't even felt anything down there. Tonight, seeing her awakened something. My clitoris was throbbing. It was the first time since getting out of the hospital that I had any feelings of the sort. I wasn't sure if I would have a return of feeling to my clitoris or those feelings you get in the pit of your stomach when you have an attraction to someone. I wasn't sure how ready I was to be intimate again, but I missed her and my body did too. I craved her touch, caress, warmth and comfort. I was very aroused and wanted to please myself. Part of me was afraid it would hurt. I didn't know what to expect. The first self-induced orgasm felt so good, I did it twice. At least I knew, that part worked just fine.

"How are you today?"

"I'm doing okay. This past week was pretty busy."

"Right you missed last week because of the dance performances. How did they go?"

"It was so good. The girls did an amazing job. We had a packed house every night. The last night my auntie came and Sarah too."

"That is nice that they showed up for you. How did it feel to see Sarah again?"

"Honestly, I was excited at first. Then, realized it may be an uncomfortable conversation."

"How did the conversation go?"

"We kept it basic. You know. Thanks for coming. The show was good. Nothing personal."

"Did you want the conversation to be personal?"

"I am not sure I had any real expectations. I was just happy she showed up."

"Do you think you will reach out to her?"

"No. I don't think so. I am still unsure of what exactly to say."

"How about just let the conversation happen."

"I will consider that. I think I anticipate everything. Or create scenarios of how I think things will go. Just like with Karen. I remember when I thought she was super sweet and then I realized that she and I were not compatible. That turned out to be a complete disaster."

"Let's unpack that."

"We met, she seemed nice and we went out a few times. Then her behavior began to change. She was slightly possessive. Then she would show up unannounced to my job. It was becoming too much.

"Is that when you decided to end the relationship with her?"

"Yes but, she didn't seem to get it. That is when the excessive calls started." By this time my eyes were welling up with tears.

"What are you feeling right now?"

"Angry. I can't believe she was stalking me and following me and then. She... she…"

"She what Kristen? What did she do?"

"She scared me. She punched me. She beat me. She raped me with a tree branch. **A TREE BRANCH**! I was bleeding. Violated. I passed out. From the torture she inflicted on me." I was having a hard time breathing.

"Take a breath. Take a breath Kristen. In through your nose and out through your mouth." Ms. Hill handed me a bottle of water from her mini refrigerator. "It is good to let your anger out about what happened. You have every right to be angry. Don't let anyone tell you that you don't.

"It comes up at the most random times. I will be fine then all of a sudden. Intrusive thoughts. I am glad the nightmares have decreased. I would be screaming and wake up Auntie Jan."

"I want you to begin writing your dreams / nightmares down when they happen. Are you having trouble sleeping?"

"Sometimes."

"Let me know if you feel like a sleep aid would be helpful. We can talk about that. How are you feeling?"

"I feel like a weight has been lifted. While I didn't want to talk about it, it felt good to let out the anger."

"That is good to hear. I will see you next week?"

"Yes ma'am." I got up and left the office to enjoy my Saturday. I decided to treat myself to lunch and indulge in a little retail therapy.

Sarah

I knew I missed Kristen, but until I saw her, I didn't realize how much. I had no desire to act on those feelings once they were apparent. Of course, Aunt Jan was convincing me that I should at least talk to Kristen. What was I to say? *You hurt me by leaving me, when all I attempted to do was be there for you.* In the midst of my indecisive inner thoughts, I called. It was now the fourth ring and I was about to hang up when she answered.

"Sarah."

"Kristen."

"How are you?"

"I'm good. Listen, I'd like to meet you for brunch tomorrow and Bourbon Street at 1pm. Are you free?"

"Yes."

"See you then." I hung up. There was no desire to begin a conversation via telephone. I wanted to end the call quickly. It was just 9pm and I was tired, but not sleepy. After lying in bed and waiting for time to pass and letting my anxiety build all night and most of the morning, I finally got up and showered to prepare to leave. A sudden excitement ensued.

It was a beautiful day out. The sun warmed my face as I stepped outside of my building. I put my shades on to protect my eyes. I was happy to be seeing her, but the hurt surfaced. The funny thing about emotions, you never know when they will come or change, but managing them is the key to living. I arrived and didn't see her. I told the hostess that I had a reservation for two but, for now, I would sit at the bar. She walked in about 10 minutes later. I paid for my beverage and walked back over to the hostess stand. We gave a quick hug and were seated in a booth.

"How are you?"

"I'm feeling good. And you?"

"I honestly am feeling a mix of emotions. I asked you here to get clarity as to why you thought us being apart was best."

"Okay, can we order first before this conversation?" I guess I came on a little strong but, I didn't want to lose my nerve either.

"Sure." I stared at the menu. I was feeling my blood boil and began breathing slowly to calm myself. We ordered. I think I should have slowed down on the drinks. I was starting in on the mimosa after two Hurricanes I had waiting at the bar. She began with small talk.

"How is Jeff?"

"He is good. I am supposed to visit next month."

"That sounds like a nice trip planned."

"I am looking forward to it. How's Aunt Jan?"

"You know her, working, cooking and caring for me."

"That sounds about right." Then the food came. The conversation shifted. "Kristen, Let's have it." I was being a bit snarky. I know it was the alcohol talking or maybe it wasn't.

"Sarah, there aren't the words to express how sorry I am that I hurt you and pushed you away."

"Find some."

"Look if you're going to be nasty, I'm going to go." That isn't what I wanted. I needed to gain control of my feelings.

"Who is being nasty? I guess being assaulted by someone's words doesn't feel good." I wanted her to understand how deep the pain ran. I really wanted to blame the alcohol, but I knew better. I tried to pipe down on the attitude.

"Sarah, I apologize again. I was hurting so much after the loss of my mother and then I felt worse because she wasn't here to comfort me through what happened. Plus, there were things I did not tell you. That ordeal caused a lot of damage to me internally."

"What do you mean?"

"Parts of the event, I don't even remember because I blacked out. I only know some of what happened because it was told to me. They detectives found three branches of a tree." She took a deep breath. "Sarah, I had tree branches shoved into me repeatedly. The bruises you saw on my face were just the beginning of it." I had a blank stare because I had no idea.

"Oh my God, I had no idea." I leaned on the table with my elbows with my hands in my head. I felt a wave a nausea.

"How could you? I didn't say anything and I knew Auntie would never break my trust and tell you either."

"That is true, she never said a word."

"I am working on these things though."

"Really? How so?"

"For one, I am in therapy." Apparently, going to therapy was helpful. I know for Kristen it was a huge step.

"Wow, that is huge for you."

"I know I am slow to act on things. I should have been honest with you. I was embarrassed. Scared of what you would think. I felt less than a woman. Before then, I never considered children and then the option was taken away from me."

"It would have been helpful Kristen if you had just talk to me."

"I understand better now. I didn't give you a right to choose. How have you been?"

"I am good, just working to complete my clinical hours. I should be done in another month."

"Sarah that is great. I am sure you are relieved."

"That is an understatement. I actually have an opportunity to be an assistant director."

"Well okay. I see you making career moves."

"Thanks. Have to take steps to further my career and build that resume."

We exited the restaurant about two hours later and I asked, "Do you want me to walk you to the train."

"I think I will be okay. I appreciate the offer though."

"Okay. I am sure we have to walk in the same direction."

"Yes, we do."

I was being weird, I know. I didn't want to end this though. It was good to have conversation with her. I was still heartbroken that she didn't tell me what happened, but I understood better now. As we walked, it was pretty quiet. My hand brushed up against hers and she reached for it.

"You realize you are holding my hand."

"Sarah, of course I do."

"I don't want to make you uncomfortable."

"I'm not. Not at all." Her hands were soft and not clammy at all. I was afraid my hands were because I was feeling nervous.

We walked another block and I needed to turn to go to my building. “I am happy I spent time with you and happy you were able to be honest with me.”

“I enjoyed myself as well.” She kissed me on the cheek.

“Well, I guess this is it.”

“It doesn’t have to be.”

“What are you saying?”

“Sarah, we can hang out.”

“You mean now or in general?”

“Whatever works for you.”

“I have no other plans. We can go back to my apartment.” What was I doing? It is New York City there are plenty of places to go and I suggest my apartment.

“Sure.” Did my ears deceive me? She agreed. We turned to walk to my building.

When we got in the elevator, you could cut the sexual tension with a knife. We were alone as we ascended. I got bold and kissed her. Instant response to my advance and this was how we started. We got in the house and the clothes came off. We made it to the bedroom. I laid her down, discovering all that had been taken from her. There were scars. I took my time to touch and caress every inch of her. I went to the place that I know makes her quiver. I then asked her.

"Are you okay?" I could feel that she was tense. It was no rush.

"I don’t think I am ready for this." While I wanted to be all over her, I respected her and could tell she wasn’t ready.

“We don’t have to.”

“Sarah, I just...”

“I’m here.”

We kissed some more. I covered her. We lay in sislence.

Part 4

Aimee & Brian

Butterflies in My Stomach

Aimee

The street was pretty desolate. The ground was damp from rainfall as my heels clicked against the sidewalk. He held my hand as he led me in front of a closed ice cream shop. We stood still and kissed. He backed me up against the building, still kissing me and using one hand to hold my face while the other found its way up my skirt. I wore no panties on date nights for quick and easy access. This made it simple for his fingers to move in and out of my moist mounds of flesh as we kissed some more. What was only a few short minutes felt like forever. He uncovered a breast and sucked while he fingered me.

"Ahhh." He knew just how to make me feel wanted and sexy. The falling rain felt so good even as it continued to down pour over us. I opened an umbrella over us for fear he would stop. You would think we drank way too much, but brick oven pizza and a shared bottle of wine didn't qualify for inebriation for us. My sister, Andrea, agreed to give us some time off.

"Damn Baby, I - am - almost - there. Ahhh." I almost lost my balance as I released.

"You okay?" He gently pulled down my skirt. He licked his finger, tasting me.

We walked to the corner and we rode home in silence. In that brief moment, my husband made me climax and made me feel sultry. It was as if he helped me find the woman he fell in love with before she became a mom.

Andrea was great with our daughter. We didn't really trust many people outside of family with her care. I appreciated the support and was glad to get out of the house. That night, it felt like we were ourselves again. It reminded me of our wild times before we were parents or even before we were married. It was a time in our history when we lived spontaneously and let the next moment worry about itself. There were vacations, parties and many wild nights. We did it all and we did it together. Then marriage came, and with that, things changed.

My husband worked long hours. It didn't bother me. I loved being with our daughter. I've always loved children; I once had a dream to open up my own daycare. But life happened and it seemed that would never happen. I was a second grade teacher, which was something I was passionate about. It meant a lot to me, giving children a solid educational foundation and teaching the whole child, even with all of that red tape that comes with teaching within a system meant to fail children of color.

We reached home to find my sister flipping through channels. She and I were very close, talked daily and shared mostly everything with each other.

"Did you two have a good time?" Andrea said as she shut off the television to turn her attention to us.

"We did, and thanks again for watching the baby." I responded, opening my arms to her for a hug.

"Anytime. You guys should get out more."

"You keep being our free babysitter and we will." Brian joked.

Releasing from our embrace, I replied, "We will try to. It was a great night."

As she prepared to leave, I used Uber to have her cab it home. We continued to talk until it arrived. I told her, "Text when you get home."

"Aimee, you can see when I reach home on your phone."

"I know, text me anyway."

"Love you sis." And she left.

Brian went upstairs to our room when my sister and I started to chat. He knew how close we were and gave us our space. Before heading to our room to finish the evening with him, I checked in on our princess. Addison was sleeping peacefully. I gently kissed her forehead and watched her sleep for a few. I entered our bedroom and began to undress. Brian came behind me and helped undress me as he nibbled on my neck. My husband was a great lover. He knew what I needed and how to give it to me. Sometimes, he was too giving.

Brian

My wife thought I was such a great lover. Truth was, I simply loved her. Aimee had given me the best parts of herself. I got her out of her clothes and laid her down on the bed. My tongue started at her navel and followed down to her yoni. Tasting her was always a pleasure. She arched her back as I lightly circled her clitoris with my tongue, taking things slow and making her want it all the more. She released the orgasm that had built up quite loudly.

"Damn, Brian." She giggled.

"You sounded like you had a demon coming out of you girl." I lifted myself up as she continued to lay on her back. I gently kissed her lips.

"Shut up. Don't wake the baby." She playfully swatted at me.

"I love you." I let myself slide into her juicy center that I had created.

"I know you do." She closed her eyes tightly as she succumbed to the pressure of my body thrusting into hers. The synchrony of our movements as one flesh had surpassed all of my other conquests. Aimee was special.

"Babe, turn around for me."

"Oh, you wanna be nasty and slap my ass?"

"You know you like it."

"Damn sure do." She turned over on all fours, arching her back with her round booty in the air and sweet and succulent vagina, waiting for me to take advantage of her. I slid in inch-by-inch, while giving her duel stimulation with my finger.

"Brian, talk dirty to me."

"Oh, so you giving all the directions tonight."

"Yeah baby, fuck this pussy like you own it."

"You know, I love this pussy." I was holding on to her waist and the dirtier the conversation got, the faster I pumped and the faster I pumped the closer I got to the orgasm I was chasing.

"Slap that ass B."

POP "You like that don't you?"

"Yeah, I love it. Make me remember why I married this dick." I was hitting it so hard she was on her stomach. Doing Kegels around my penis, making me lose control. And just like that, I couldn't hold on to my soldiers. They were in forward motion.

"Baby, I am. Shit. Shit. Shit."

"Brian, lower your voice. You are going to wake the baby."

I got up and went to our bathroom to clean up. Aimee of course came in behind me, took care of herself and then went to check on our princess.

My wife and I met in college our senior year. Aimee was from New York City and I was trying to get there. The irony.

"Aren't you an education major?" I asked. I was finally able to spark up a conversation with her. Every time I saw her, I backed down.

"Yeah, so?" She looked me up and down with her arms folded. That New York attitude was on ten.

"I hardly ever see you anymore." Out of nowhere, the nape of my neck became hot and my nerves were getting the better of me.

"What do you mean anymore? Have you been watching me?" She gave me a face that looked like she just sucked a lemon. "That's creepy." She turned on her heels to walk away.

I reached for her arm to keep her from leaving. She swung around and shot me a look that said *get your hands off me*.

I let go. "No. I just remember seeing you during lunch more often with your girls and lately, I haven't."

I dated a few girls during my college career, but no one I wanted to take home to meet my mother. After getting to know Aimee, I saw she was different because she loved God and her family.

"Where you been hiding yourself?" I felt the heat rising and from my neck.

"I haven't been hiding and if you must know, I am student teaching."

"That means you are off campus every day?"

"You catch on quick." She moved to walk away after that comment. I still had more to say, so I walked with her. All the way to her dorm room we talked. She was interesting. Apparently, she wanted to open a quality preschool of her own and planned to get her master's in education. When we got to her door, I'd hoped I would be invited in. That did not happen. It was a school night. We exchanged information from there.

We moved to her hometown after graduation. I visited, but that was different from living there. While I was from Maryland, it was still the suburbs. I quickly learned to maneuver the city. After living in a crappy one bedroom in the South Bronx, we finally settled down in Harlem. We scraped together all our money and bought a split-level condominium in Hamilton Heights. Aimee went to church down the hill from the house.

I visited the church with her several times and I liked it well enough. The people were friendly and her family attended, so I got to know many of the people fairly quickly. At home, my mother went to church regularly. I would go with her for Mother's Day, Easter and New Year's Eve. I would also show up for her special occasions. Once I went away for college, she didn't force church on me anymore. I believed in God, but being a member and participating on a regular basis was something I never committed myself to. Aimee never forced church on me either and I appreciated that. She embodied a Christ-like spirit. She was kind, forgiving, showed love to any and every one she met, especially her students.

Aimee

When he first moved here with me from school, Brian was a fish out of water. I believed it was destiny for him to live here. He came, he saw, and he conquered. He went back to school to get his MBA and up the corporate ladder he went. I received my Masters in Education and we both did what we loved. I was proud of our accomplishments. We stuck to our goals.

We entertained often in our new home. We didn't need a reason to celebrate or have people over. Our second big event was a beautiful spring day in May, right after we were married. We had drinks and food. There was laughter, family and friends surrounding us. My boy Darius and I were talking and laughing as we always do. We have been friends since childhood. He's always been there for me. In the middle of our conversation, Brian interrupted us.

"Babe, can I talk to you?" He smiled at me then turned to Darius. "You don't mind, do you Darius?"

"Nah bro. She is all yours."

I asked him what was going on, but he didn't answer. He held my hand as I followed him upstairs into the bedroom. I thought he was trying to take advantage of a little private time. I was completely wrong.

WHAM!

Out of nowhere, his hand went across my face. I stumbled backward to the wall, breaking my fall. Standing square in front of me, I thought he was going to do it again.

"You think it is okay to disrespect me in front of my face, in my home and in front of our guests?" He said through tight lips.

I held my face. It was hot and the pain slowly crept in. With my vision blurred with tears, I was able to get out my next words very slowly.

"What...what. are. you. talking. about? I was entertaining our guests."

"You were entertaining one guest, Darius. Do you think I'm blind? I watched you two the entire time. You were laughing and touching his arm and shoulder. Are the two of you comedians now? Stay away from him." He barked. Then stepped away to look into the mirror to smooth out his shirt.

He demanded. "Get yourself together and return to the party."

The feeling like I had just been struck with a ton of bricks was the only way to explain how I felt in that moment. I was completely dumbfounded. He had never showed any signs of being abusive. At least none I could remember. We shared a bank account, but he never denied me access. We had arguments, but nothing major. It was like someone flipped a switch. I went into the bathroom and peered into the mirror. My face was still hot, but nothing physical to suggest I was wacked in the face by my loving husband. Before returning to the party as Brian demanded, I retouched my makeup. Involuntary tears were released from my eyes streaking my cheek. Back downstairs in the parlor, I saw both my friend, Darius and my husband. I chose my sister.

"Aimee, what's wrong?" She had worried look on her face.

"Nothing. I am fine. I could use another drink though." My mind had yet to fully process what just happened and a drink would surely calm my nerves.

"I know you, my sister. What's wrong?" She pressed me, but I wasn't going to let up on any information about what had happened moments before.

"Andrea, leave it be." I made my way to the drinks and poured myself a glass of wine. I saw Brian talking to his best friend, Mike, but he was watching me the entire time. I smiled at him as best I could. It felt as if I entered an alternative universe. Here I am trying to convince myself, my family and friends that all was well, when clearly, they were not.

When everyone left, I was afraid. I went in the bathroom and cried. Then he came to me lifted my face in his hands and told me he would never again put his hands on me in a hurtful way. I believed him. Then on the bathroom floor, he spread my legs, lifted my buttocks and tasted my yoni. He licked and sucked on my center until I shook. With tears in my eyes, I made no sound. My heart was overwhelmed with confusion. I had so many questions going through my head. *How could he love me, but put his hands on me like that? When did he become this person?*

Brian

I didn't mean to do it. I wasn't sure what came over me. I just didn't like how Darius, her "friend," was all over her. A guy knows when his woman is being hit on. That was something I wasn't about to tolerate. I did not want to have her misunderstand how I felt, so I made it clear with my actions. I made her breakfast in bed hoping she would accept my peace offering.

"Good morning Aimee." I entered our room with a tray of food and drink.

"Good morning." She grumbled, waking up to the calling of her name.

"I made breakfast." I moved her cellphone from the nightstand to sit the tray on it.

"Thank you." She sat up in bed and looked at the spread on her plate.

Her responses were very dry. I knew I had lots to make up for.

"We have lemon zinger tea, your favorite. Eggs, bacon extra crispy, toast with butter and strawberry jam and a strawberry mango mesclun salad."

"Brian this is lovely, but you didn't have to do this."

"I wanted to do this." I handed her the hot cup of tea. She seemed hesitant to take it.

"Where is yours?" Blowing the steam away from the cup she took a sip.

"I am going to go out for a run. I'll eat later."

I kissed her and I could feel the stiffness in her lips, her body rigid. I knew I had to make more of an overture to smooth this over. It was still bugging me how Darius was all over her. I was trying to put it out of my mind. Aimee had never given anyone other than me so much attention. The shit was driving me crazy. They were friends since childhood, yes, but he was drooling all over her. Hanging on her every word. Laughing at every joke. I wasn't comfortable with their friendship but, this dude was like family. Every function he was invited to and he would show up. Sometimes he would arrive alone or sometimes with a woman, he never failed to make an appearance. It was making me incensed all over again. I went for a run to clear my head and the ended up traveling further downtown to pick up a nice piece of jewelry for Aimee. That should do it.

Aimee

Brian thought that breakfast in bed was the cure to this. I'd heard about domestic violence situations. How women don't leave and continue to let their partners hurt them. I couldn't imagine that this was about to be my life. He wasn't withholding money or keeping me from my family. He was just a little jealous. Right? Brian said he wouldn't do it again. Right? I begged, "God, please let this cup pass from me. I am not sure where I went wrong or why this is happening. I genuinely love my husband but, I don't want to be physically hurt anymore. Amen."

It was Sunday and I got myself together to get ready for church. Andrea was the first person I saw when I walked up to our church. Because we are tight, I didn't know how long I could keep up the charade with her. Andrea and I are the definition of the saying, my sister is my best friend. She would be the wrong person to know any of this. I was older by three years, but she had always taken care of me. Between the two of us, I was more laid back and definitely more square than she.

"Hey big sis."

"Hey my sister, how are you today?" We kissed each other on the cheek.

"Aimee, I should be asking you that."

"I'm good."

"You would tell me if you were in trouble, right?"

"Of course. But, I'm okay." The lying had begun. The phrase *I'm okay* was the beginning of me silencing myself. I had to learn to break out of that and speak my truth. So many times, *I'm okay* was my reply to the question *how are you, but* I was not.

Today it seemed like everyone was speaking to me, specifically God. Pastor's sermon was from *Philippians 4:6-7Do not be anxious about anything, but in every situation, by prayer and petition, with thanksgiving, present your requests to God. And the peace of God, which transcends all understanding, will guard your hearts and your minds in Christ Jesus.* The title of the sermon was Pray, in all Things". The spirit of the Lord was speaking to me and the tears streamed down my face. Andrea passed me a tissue.

After church my cousin, Liza, Andrea and I were congregating.

"The party was great last night. When do you plan to finish up the room off the kitchen?" Liza asked.

"I don't know, we have spent so much already."

"What's up with you? You seem distracted." Liza glared at me.

"Yeah, tell us sis, what's up with you?" I could feel that Andrea knew, even though I knew she didn't, but that was our connection.

"I promise, I'm fine." I shifted my weight from left to right. I was uncomfortable with all the questions and did not want to be found out.
Thankfully, Liza decided to shift the conversation, "I'm going to have a girls' night next week. Are you guys going to come?" Liza asked.

My response was quick, "I'm in." I didn't want to hem and haw over it. That would have made things even more suspect.

"Me too." Drea chimed in.

"Good, I'm kicking Josh and the kids out for the night. Just bring a bottle of wine or two. I got the menu all figured out."

Things seemed to be back to normal between Brian and I. Letting my guard down and just a week after the first incident occurred. We were watching a movie and my phone buzzed.

"Who is texting at this hour?" He never tripped about text or calls. This seemed to be new. I looked at my phone. It was Liza. Another came right after."

"It's Liza."

"What does she want?" He barked.

"Just asking me to come a little early tomorrow to help set up."

The good thing was that he didn't know that there was a second text, from Darius. I tried to keep our friendship as quiet as possible. My friendship with Darius had never seemed to be an issue previously. Maybe it was and Brian never said anything. I didn't know what changed for him. He was my friend, like a brother to me. After the movie, I went to bed. My bladder woke me up and I opened my eyes to Brian was standing over me.

"You lying bitch."

BAM. He hit me and then snatched me out of bed.

"Liza texting. Just Liza, huh?" He threw me down. My back hit the nightstand.

"I see you didn't understand when I told you to stay away from Darius." I attempted to fight him off, that made it worse. He started kicking me in my back over and over and I just stayed in a fetal position waiting for it to stop.

"You think you can beat me; you think you going to try to hit me back. Bitch, I am the man around here." He finally stopped as I wailed out in pain from the last blow. Then yelled, "Go fix yourself."

I couldn't move from that position, no matter how hard I tried. In shock, feeling like I had a mountain dropped on me, I just stayed curled into a ball, crying in silence. I heard him go downstairs, he was still yelling, but I wasn't exactly sure what he was saying. I used the sheets to lift myself up off the floor. I crawled in bed. The pulsating pain in my lower back to my buttocks made me pass out.

This was the first time I had to cancel on my family or friends, skip church or call out of work because I needed to heal. I couldn't be seen in public with bruises and scars. I took pictures. I didn't know why. Maybe one day I would need proof or maybe to remind myself of what was actually happening. When I finally awoke, I hobbled to the bathroom. My lower back was black and blue. There was a gash where my back hit the nightstand. I climbed in the shower and the water hitting an open wound made me yell. I then cried silent tears washing my pain down the drain.

God,

If you are listening please help me. I don't know what I did to deserve this. I really thought Brian loved me but, this can't be love. This isn't what I have seen expressed between my parents and other family members. God, save me.

Brian

Why doesn't she understand that I want her all to myself? She made me do this to her. I told her to stay away from that nigga. She didn't fucking listen. Why wouldn't she just fucking listen? Do as I say. I gave her all that I could. We traveled, partied and now we had a home and I made her my wife. What didn't she understand? She is all mine. I'd been a little stressed with work and all these new bills. I just needed my wife to understand me. She should fucking understand.

The next day, I didn't even say anything to her. I went and ordered a fruit bouquet and had it sent to the house. Then I went to the gym. My boy Mike was there. We had been friends since college, too. We also pledged together.

"Brian, what's up? You going hard over there." Mike greeted me with a fist pump. I guess the stress was showing.

"Nah, I'm good."

"You sure? You hitting them weights hard."

"I said, I'm good." I wanted him to stop trying to engage me in conversation.

"You want to hang when we done?"

"Not today. Got to get home to the wife, but let's get up soon."

I didn't intend to be so short with my friend. I mean, we've been tight for so long but his questions were irritating. Or maybe I felt guilty. I don't know what was happening with me. My demeanor spoke louder than I could because he finally let me be and I finished my workout.

About fifteen minutes later I announced. "Bro, I'm out." I threw my towel around my neck.

"I will get up with you later then. Tell Aimee I said hey."

"Will do." I gave him a pound and went in the locker room. I opened my locker grabbed what I needed for a shower. The steam from the shower felt good, but I didn't want to linger. I needed to get home to my wife.

When I got home, Aimee was still in bed. Since I was showered, I got in bed with her. I went to spoon her and she shrieked. I guess she didn't want me near her.

"Are you sore? Do you want me to draw you an Epsom salt bath?"

"No."

"Okay, I will just lay here with you."

She didn't say anything, but I could hear her whimpering.

That evening, I ordered from her favorite restaurant, LoLo's, shark and bake seafood dish, durty rice and Johnny cakes. I made drinks to go with our dinner. We ate in silence; it was so quiet you could hear a pin drop. I could see she was hesitant to drink. I guess I was hoping to get her inhibitions to come down a bit. At my urging, she began to drink alcohol like she was sipping water. That seemed to work. She was talking a little bit more. Not about anything of significance. At least she wasn't sitting in silence.

Aimee

That day while he was out, I started writing in a journal because who could I possibly tell that this was happening to me. I needed some kind of outlet. The scripture from pastor's sermon became my favorite and helped me daily.

I wrote the scripture before writing anything else.

Philippians 4:6-7. Do not be anxious about anything, but in every situation, by prayer and petition, with thanksgiving, present your requests to God. And the peace of God, which transcends all understanding, will guard your hearts and your minds in Christ Jesus.

I am not sure what is going on here. Things have changed so much. I thought I knew him. We had been together for over four years and then got married. Now This! I just feel so raw. God, if you are listening, please help me. We have this home and I just don't have any idea of what to do. I can't tell my family. They all love him and they would be mortified if I told them. I don't know why, but I took pictures of the scars he left me with. Maybe I will find the strength to press charges. Who am I kidding? It is just embarrassing that I allowed this to even happen. Everyone thinks I am so strong, what will they think if they knew this about me?

the inevitability

Bound to happen.
Hurt
Deceit
Lies you told me.
I believed
I trusted that what you uttered from your lips to me was genuine.

The Gospel.
My Love, I will never...
Not again.
Then BANG!
My head
My face
My arms
My heart
Bruised
Beat
Battered
It was bound to happen
Calling me your BITCH
Stupid again
The struggle for power.
Honeymoon Stage
Over.
I need divine protection.
Before the inevitable happens.

I am not sure for me what the inevitable could be, but I don't think I want to find out either. I wasn't sure how to get myself to a point of accepting that my husband, dare I say... is abusive. Physically abusive. Verbally abusive. My father never called me anything, but my name. Yes, my parents argued, had disagreements, but nothing like this. What did I miss with Brian? I even considered taking my own life. I stood in the bathroom and contemplated slitting my wrists. And just like that I realized I wasn't going to give him the satisfaction.

To keep me under his thumb, he continued to use sex, food and presents as a way to apologize for his actions. This seemed like forever ago, but it continually happened. I wrote in my journal and documented every verbal and physical occurrence of violence. I was very careful to always keep it with me. I didn't want him to find it and give him another reason to wail on me. It was my own personal thoughts and feelings. It became my sanctuary.

I learned really well how to hide my pain, physical and emotional, in plain sight. Changing appointments, wearing clothing to cover up. I went to work one time and my arm was bruised. One of my close co-workers, Rodriguez (we use each other's last names), tapped my shoulder one day and I nearly jumped out of my skin.

"Brooks, you okay?"

"Yeah, I am okay." There it was again. Clearly, I was not, but when folks ask *how are you?* Did they really want to know how you were? Or were those just pleasantries? I couldn't even begin to find the words to say how I was feeling or doing.

"You seem super jumpy lately. I just touched your shoulder."

"I'm good. I could probably use more sleep. Other than that, I'm okay."

"You coming to the holiday party?"

"I want to but, I am not sure."

Rodriguez knew, but he didn't want to pry. I could tell he was worried about me. One day, Brian came to my job. While he didn't do anything to embarrass me at my work, Rodriguez, whom he had met previously and I were working on something for our students.

"Hi. What are you doing here?" I said, uncomfortable and nervous he would make a scene.

"I thought we could go to dinner." Brian said.

"Luis, you remember Brian?"

"Yeah, how you doing man?" They shook hands.

"Good. You?" Brian replied very dryly.

"Good."

"I can't go just yet; we have work to finish up." I said.

"I can wait." He was being really weird. It seemed like any man was a threat.

"It will be a while. Just go home and I will see you later." This is where I thought that things would go left, but Brian reluctantly left.

Rodriguez asked questions. "That was awkward. What's going on with the two of you? You are always jumpy. You are wearing long sleeves when it is fairly warm. You don't seem like yourself." Rodriguez began to pry, not taking no for an answer.

"Nothing."

"We talk. I think we know one another pretty well. We are friends, Aimee. You would tell me if something was wrong."

"Of course. You and I are friends and yes, I would tell you if something was wrong." More lies.

"So, tell me, because you seem to be very

uncomfortable around your husband and that is alarming."

"There isn't anything to tell. He just gets jealous sometimes is all."

I wanted to tell Rodriguez everything, but something was stopping me from being completely honest. I didn't want him to think less of me.

"Is it more than just jealousy? Has he put his hands on you?" I wanted to say yes.

"No, nothing like that." I felt bad for lying, but I couldn't tell him the truth.

"If you need to talk, come to my house and stay or anything, please don't hesitate."

I have so many people who love me and still, I couldn't say a word. It was like slowly someone was taking pieces of my heart. Shredding my soul. It did not feel like much was left anymore. Neither physically, mentally, emotionally, spiritually. There were times when I was like if God loved me why would he allow this to happen to me.

Our home went from two unhappy people to a happy couple with a beautiful princess. We were now a family of three. I felt like my pregnancy with Addison saved me. Not once did he put his hands on me during my pregnancy. I thought that the nightmare I was living for the last three years was over. I still prayed and recited:

Philippians 4:6-7. Do not be anxious about anything, but in every situation, by prayer and petition, with thanksgiving, present your requests to God. And the peace of God, which transcends all understanding, will guard your hearts and your minds in Christ Jesus.

I was anxious often because I thought every day he would go back to his abusive behavior. This was the longest time since the abusive behavior again that he kept his hands off. I was so thankful that Addison was here. I felt like God sent her to save me and my marriage.

Until, the honeymoon phase was yet over, yet again. Addison and I were home, playing, with the movie *Sing* in the background. She liked music. I was in love in another way. Addison was beautiful. Of course, you think your child is cute, but she was. I wasn't sure I was in love with Brian. I loved him, but *in love* was questionable. How could he love me? I asked that question often. Not after the things he did, he couldn't. It was around eight o'clock in the evening he walked in drunk.

"Hey Brian, how was your day?" I inquired in an attempt to be the wife I always wanted to be for him.

"Fine," he snarled. Flopping down on the sofa in front of the television, he kicked his feet up on the ottoman. Letting out a loud belch, he seemed uninterested in me and his daughter.

"I left you dinner on the stove." I got up to give him a kiss with the baby in my arms. He moved his head to keep me from kissing his lips. He didn't even acknowledge that Addison was close to him, too.

"Brian, did you hear me? I left dinner on the stove for you."

"I heard you. Stop yelling and turn that shit off." I put Addison down.

"Are you okay?"

"I would be if you would shut the fuck up."

I walked away, picked Addison back up and went up the stairs. I put Addison down in her crib. I could see where this had the potential to go and I didn't want my daughter to be privy to this. It was bad enough he was cursing in front of her like a sailor. I went back down to get her bottle with the baby monitor in my hand. Brian had my phone in his hand.

"What are you doing?" I asked.

"Why is he texting you?"

"He who?"

"Darius, that is who."

"He is my friend. There is nothing happening there, as I've said so many times. He was asking when he could come see Addy."

POW!

All I could think was *here we go again.* Brian's hand connected with my jaw so much that my head began to throb. I screamed out in anguish, holding my busted lip. Then…I heard my baby crying. That was jarring. I tried to shake it off, but my ear was ringing. Still raging, he followed me to the kitchen. Out of nowhere, I felt another blow from behind to the middle of my back, I crumbled to the floor. I looked up at him holding a rolling pin.

I screamed, "Brian, leave me alone. I need to get Addison."

I guess he finally realized he should stop. He turned around and went in the living room and started watching television. It sounded like her cries got louder the more I climbed the stairs. My head hurt and the ringing in my left ear seemed louder but, I needed to get to my baby. The pain in my back hurt with every breath I took. As I was reaching the top, I grabbed my chest, the pain radiating in my back.

With tears in my eyes I fed Addison, laid her down and waited in her room for Brian to fall asleep. He was so drunk it didn't take very long. I called my cousin, Liza.

"Liza, can me and the baby come by?"

"Yeah. Why are you whispering?" I could hear her moving the phone around.

"I will call you from the car."

I quickly hung up, packed a bag for myself and for the baby and headed out the front door to the car. Thankfully, it was only a few paces from the house considering all I was carrying. One of my neighbors saw me leaving and I prayed she would just say hello and not attempt to have a long conversation.

"Hey Aimee."

"Fine. Just fine."

"Need some help there?"

"No, I'm good." Thankfully she didn't ask anymore. Once Addison was in, I jumped in the driver's seat, buckled my seatbelt and got out of there as fast as I could.

I called Liza back and as soon as she answered, "Hello," I began to cry.

"Liza, I am in the car." It felt good to get it out.

"What is going on? Why are you crying?"

"Liza, I need to get there. I'm exhausted. I can't live like this anymore and now with Addison. We will talk when I get there."

All the way, I just listened to *I'm Still Standing* on repeat as I cried.

When I pulled up, Liza immediately opened the door.

"Josh, come quick." She turned to face the inside of her home. "Help with this stuff." Josh came and helped us with our bags. Liza took Addison from me and we sat down in the living room. Josh and Liza took one look at my face and that was the beginning of the questions. I had no choice but to respond as best I could. I was just glad the kids were gone for the weekend. Explaining to adults is one thing, to children would be an entirely different ballgame.

"What happened?" Liza asked.

"How long has this been happening? I'm going to kill him." Josh said.

They were firing questions so fast I could barely get an answer out between tears. Liza took Addison in the guest room to lay down and came back out. Josh was pacing the floor as Liza and I spoke. I guess I didn't realize he hit me in my eye with the adrenaline rush but, I could now feel it was swollen.

"Put this on your eye." Liza said as she handed me an ice pack.

"I am so ashamed and embarrassed. I didn't want my baby to get hurt."

"How long Aimee?" Josh asked again.

"Well, it hasn't happened in a long time," was all I could muster up as an answer.

"How long?" I could see Josh was ready to go back to the city and whip his ass.

"It started the day of the party." Looking at my cousin become angrier with my lack of response, I decided to be open and honest about the last few years.

"What party?" Liza said.

I shifted my eyes downward as I said, "The housewarming."

"Wait, that was over three years ago. Aimee, three years." Liza, said putting up three fingers on her right hand in the air to emphasize her point.

"Yeah, I don't know. He thought that something was happening with Darius."

"Darius? That's ridiculous. You have been friends forever. He's family." Josh said.

"That's what I told him and he felt that Darius was hitting on me. He said he would never do it again. That wasn't true."

Liza and I were talking and Josh was pacing.

"Who else knows?" Liza asked cautiously.

"Nobody. People have suspected but, that's all." I was afraid to be honest, but I couldn't hold on to it anymore. It was killing my soul and my body was hurting. I don't want my baby to see me like this. How can I be someone for her to look up to? That night, I barely slept. My head was pounding, my back was sore, my heart was hurting and my face was throbbing.

It was Saturday morning. I woke up and almost forgot where I was. I smelled breakfast and remembered I was at Liza's. The baby wasn't in the bed with me. Liza must have come to get her. I just lay in the bed. Staring at the ceiling… waiting… to hear God speak. I prayed... waited for answers. The answers that did not come right away. My heart was overwhelmed with sadness for myself. I sat up, reached in my purse and opened my journal to write.

Reasons to Love Me
Can count more than three
I can love me unlimited
For my personality
and for my sheer grace

Then there's the trinity
Spiritual, Physical, Mental
All growing daily
There is one stronger than the other
But even I can't choose

When all three are not in sync
Not working together
I am not me made from thee…
God
Reasons to love me
Even if my mother does
It can't be more than me

Depressed
Loving
Everybody
But me
Not knowing how special I can be.

I feel lost and abandoned. No one knew what he does after he loves me. He sometimes comes home so angry. The sunglasses collection is growing. Now that Liza and Josh know, I am not sure what will happen. I couldn't put my baby in danger, that I knew. I already feel the shit hitting the fan. I am afraid to turn my phone on. I can only imagine how many times he has called, and how many messages he has left. Text and voicemail for that matter. How do I return to our home? Do I give him more chances? Do I walk away? He has said time and time again, he wouldn't, he was apologetic, he loved me. I don't know this to be love.

When I finally got up, I brushed my teeth and washed my face. I threw on my robe over my PJs. What I wasn't expecting was Andrea to be there at the table. I was not ready for this.

"Good morning." I said, not knowing what the response would be.

"Your face?" Andrea got up and moved to me. Gently taking my face into her hands she began to weep.

"When did you get here? Liza, why did you tell her?" My anger was misplaced, that I was aware of. I wasn't ready to face everyone I loved about what I was dealing with.

"A few hours ago. Why didn't you tell me?" Andrea retorted.

"What would you have me say? Oh, by the way, my husband has been beating me up regularly. That's why I missed church today. I was embarrassed, hurt, heartbroken. I didn't want anyone to see me like this. I didn't know I was this weak of a woman. I felt foolish, like I got played. I didn't know how to get out of it. I thought we got passed it with Addison being born."

By that time, I was crying so hard and allowed myself to fall apart in the safety, and loving care of my family. I could barely breathe between trying to talk and crying. My cousin and my sister just hugged me. Addison was in her pack-and-play sleeping. I finally got myself together.

"You need a plan." Liza said.

"What am I supposed to do?"

"Aimee, this isn't you. I have known you your entire life and you have always stood up for yourself." Liza said.

"This is different, he is my husband." I defended our marriage knowing good and well I shouldn't. I'm his wife. Wasn't I supposed to defend our marriage and him?

Before either of them could offer up a rebuttal, my phone rang. I looked at the screen and it was Darius. I didn't answer. I declined the call and sent him to voicemail. It rang again… It was Darius.

"Is it Brian?" Andrea said, sounding like she was ready for a fight.

"No, it is Darius."

"Answer it." They said in unison. I was afraid to answer it. He doesn't ever call me back to back like this. I hope he doesn't know what is going on. Darius loves me in a way that a brother loves a sister.

I took a deep breath and finally answered the phone. "Hey, what's up?"

"I was calling you because we were supposed to go have brunch, but you haven't been answering. I wanted to make sure you were okay, so I stopped by your house and before I could even get to the door, Brian came out and was accusing me of trying to get with you. Where are you?" He sounded very worried.

"Darius, I am so sorry. I completely forgot. I am at Liza's house."

"Why are you there? What is going on, that you are not telling me?" He said.

"Please believe me, I am okay", It is habitual. Saying *I am okay* when I am not. Once the words fell from my lips, I got an acrid taste in my mouth. Andrea and Liza just gave me the death glare.

"Right now, I believe nothing you are saying to me. I am coming to Liza's."

"No, that isn't…" Before I could finish my sentence, he had hung up. I excused myself and went to shower. When I came back out, I picked up my Addy and took her to breastfeed. That bought me more time to avoid conversation. After I put Addy down, I had to go back out and face the music. They didn't hear me coming. I stood there and listened.

"How long has she been going through this?" Darius said.

"Seems like from the beginning of the marriage." Josh replied.

"I thought my sister and I were closer than this." Andrea sounded like she was crying.

"I guess she was embarrassed and felt she could get through it on her own." Liza said.

I heard Darius talking about stopping by my house and Brian acting like a fool.

I finally walked in the room to hear how Brian was acting towards him. Darius jumped up and took one look at me and his face turned grim.

"What the…" Before he could finish. I said.

"Darius, I am okay." That taste returned to my mouth. It was almost as if my body was having a visceral reaction to my lying.

"Your face isn't okay." His jaw was clenched and fists were balled up.

"Andrea, can you keep the baby the rest of the weekend? I need to go home." I asked knowing all hell would break loose when I did.

"Go home?" It was a chorus of voices.

"Yes, go home. We are still married."

"You are not going alone." Darius said.

Josh agreed, "I don't think that is a good idea. If he lays his hands on you again. I will have to lay his ass out."

"If any of you show up with me, it will be worse for me later on."

"Andrea, not a word of this to mom and dad."

"For now." She said snidely.

Brian

She just left. I didn't have any idea as to where she was. I called, I texted. I called her parents and she had not even spoken to them. Where did she go? This time, I thought I had completely alienated her. Not only did she leave, but my daughter was with her. How could she take my child and not tell me where she is going? I wanted to call her sister, but I then realized that she may now know and I didn't want to have that conversation per se. I can't believe this; Darius had the audacity to come to my doorstep. I knew they were doing something. My mind was going in several directions and then I heard the door. She came back to me.

"Aimee, where were you? I was worried." I walked over to hug her, but she put up her hands to stop me from getting too close.

"Look, I did not come back to replay last night. I went to Liza's because I needed to not be in the same space with you."

"In the same space, what the fuck does that mean?"

"Brian, look at my face. You did all this with Addison in earshot. I don't want my child subjected to this kind of behavior."

"Where are you going now?" I followed her like a puppy following its master after getting in trouble.

"Don't worry, I will be back on Monday. Addison is with Andrea."

"Excuse me, I am your husband. where are you going?" I grabbed her arm. I had no control. The urge was so strong to have her face meet my fist. I can't even say it was the alcohol this time, I was completely sober. I followed her into the kitchen.

"Let go of me, Brian." She yanked her arm for me to loosen my grip, but I didn't; I wouldn't. She needed to know I was still in control.

"You hoe, you must be going to stay with Darius. Is that why he rolled up to my door looking for you? You fucking him now?" I gripped her arm even tighter.

"I already told you to let go of me. You're being ridiculous. I'm doing no such thing."

"You lying bitch."

BAM!

My hand landed across her face and blood flew out of her mouth. Her body fell over in half onto the stove. I turned my back on her telling her who I was in this house as I began walking away. I heard her mumble something, but when I spun around to ask her to repeat it… ***BAM!***

The next thing I knew I had a bad headache, she hit me with a cast iron pan. I was stunned and that was the last thing I remember. When I came to, she'd left.

My head was throbbing, worse than a bad headache. I wasn't about to go to the hospital. I just pulled myself together, showered, took a BC Powder and got dressed to go to the gym. I called to see if Mike would be there.

"Bro, what you up to?"

"Getting dressed." Mike replied.

"Can you meet me at the gym?"

"What's up?"

"I just need to talk."

"I will be there in 20 minutes."

I was at the gym; the headache was slightly there still. Instead of doing weights, I decided to jump on the treadmill. I felt like I was running without a purpose. What I was running to or what I was running from, I didn't know. But it was helping me to think about my actions, the mess I created. I was ready to admit that much. I needed a judgment free zone. I knew Mike would be that person. He was frat.

"Hey, you ready to hit the weights." Mike said. I didn't even see him come in.

"Yeah."

"What's up? You were in a zone on the treadmill." My stomach was in knots. I honestly did not know what Mike would say. He was friends with Aimee too. I just don't know how he would react.

"I was just thinking a lot. Aimee and I have been having problems." I wasn't completely honest with him. I couldn't tell him that I was the sole cause of the problems. Truth be told, Aimee was a great wife.

"Sorry to hear that. What's happening?"

"I think she is cheating on me."

"Aimee? She would never."

I can't believe he said this. Whose side was he on? I knew I couldn't trust him once he said that.

"Aimee is the most loyal and loving woman. She has always been there for you. Plus, with Addison, I can't imagine. She would want to keep things all intact. You know, the family unit. Sis is big on family and her belief in God. I just can't imagine her cheating on you."

"I hear you talking, but she keeps texting and talking to that Darius dude. I am not feeling it. He is always around."

"I hear you, but you have to respect the relationship. They have been friends for years. Like brother and sister. Again, I don't see Aimee stepping out on you. She has been with you during the worst and best times."

We finished our workout session then decided to go for drinks to continue talking about my problems. During the conversation, I realized how embarrassing it would be to tell my closest friend that I have been hitting my wife. I left Mike and went home. I didn't really want to be there, but where else was I going to go? I knew I would be going home to an empty house. Talking to my mom would be great right now although, she was the last person I could bring myself to talk to. She would know something was wrong and I could not risk that. Then, my phone rang and it was my mother. Why was it that women seemed to have this sixth sense? My lying started all over again that day. Not that I was being fully honest to begin with.

"Hi mom."

"Hello son. How are you?" In that moment, I missed her being close.

"I'm good."

"Where are my granddaughter and Aimee?"

"Ummm, they went out to visit her cousin." I didn't lie to her. I just kept out the reason why she was there...which was essentially lying by omission.

"You don't sound so sure. Is everything okay?"

God, why does she know me so well? I needed to end this call as quickly as possible.

"Things are fine mom. I have to go take care of a few things."

"When are you all coming down for a visit? I miss you guys and I am sure Addy is getting so big, so fast. I love that Aimee sends me pictures. It makes me feel included. Or maybe I could come up. I would love to see her parents too."

"That is a great idea, mom. I am glad that she is sending pictures of Addy and FaceTiming." Still trying to end the conversation. "I have some work to do. I will give you a call and talk to Aimee about visiting soon."

"Any particular reason you are rushing me off the phone? You can't be that busy that you can't talk to your mom. How are you really doing?" There she goes again with the sixth sense. Mother's intuition, I guess.

"Mom, I am not trying to rush you off the phone and I already told you, I am okay. I just have a lot of work that I have to get done and I am on a deadline. In order for me to stay at the top of my game, I have to meet the demands. That includes getting the work in on time."

"Well, I will just have to FaceTime Aimee so I can see Addison like I have been doing."

"Maybe not today."

"Well, why not?"

"Mom, she is at her cousin's house. I am sure she won't be able to stop her visit to talk."

"If you say so. I will text first. Love you son."

"Love you too mom." She knew something was up. This wasn't the first time I had to lie to my mother in the last few years. Tell her why Aimee couldn't talk or why we couldn't visit.

She was supposed to visit one weekend and Aimee and I had one of our episodes. It was a pretty nasty one. It was so bad, she had to go to the ER. That was very uncomfortable because they ask so many questions.

"Mrs. Brooks. How did this happen?" The nurse was jotting down some notes when she asked her about how her injury occurred.

"I slipped and fell down my stairs." Of course, she had to lie, again. She wouldn't dare inform them that I had taken a Louisville slugger to her arm and legs. She could not move her left arm.

"That was a nasty fall. We will stitch up this wound here and send you to x-ray. It seems like you may have broken your arm."

I stepped out to go to the bathroom and I saw the nurse went to speak with Aimee. I tried to get back as soon as possible. When I returned to the room, I heard her talking to Aimee. I stood outside the curtain to listen to what they were saying.

"If he is hurting you, you can tell us. We can have social worker come down to speak with you."

"No thank you."

"I know you don't know me. I see the physical pain you are in and the pain in your face. Things happen and there is no need to be embarrassed, but you do not have to stay and you don't deserve this either."

Was she telling my wife to leave me? That is when I stopped the conversation and joined Aimee. The nurse stopped talking. They both looked up at me as if surprised I was there.

"Thank you, Nurse Carol. I appreciate your help." Amiee said speaking to the nurse, head and eyes lowered.

"Yes, thanks Carol." I added in.

The nurse responded with her eyes fixed on Amiee. "You're welcome. I'm glad to help. You will need to spend six weeks in the cast. Take ibuprofen for the pain and follow up with Dr. Weinfeld, the orthopedic doctor."

She told her she would and then the nurse left. Shortly after Amiee was taken to x-ray by transport, it was almost another 45 minutes for a doctor from the orthopedic department to come see her.

The doctor said, "Sir, if you would like to grab some food for the two of you, you can. This will take some time."

"No, I am good. I can wait."

"Honey, I can use a ginger ale."

"Fine, I will be back." It was making me paranoid that people kept trying to get me to leave the room. What are they saying to her when I am not there? I didn't trust them. Especially that nurse, Carol. She kept coming in asking Aimee if she was okay and how was her pain.

When I got back to the room, there looked like there was some progress.

"Finally. It looks like we can leave soon."

"About another 15 minutes."

About 4 hours later, she was discharged.

When we got home, she just went into the tv room and sat in the chair. I hated when she stopped speaking to me. The silence was deafening. It felt disrespectful.

"What was that nurse saying to you? You know, what's her name? Carol."

"Nothing, she was just asked me if I was okay. If I needed anything, you know, pain medication."

"Oh, so you going to just lie to my face?" Before I realized what I was doing, I picked up the remote and hit her in the forehead with it.

"I am telling the truth." She raised her arm with the cast to block me from hitting her, again.

"Aimee, I was listening to the conversation and you are a lying bitch."

"Brian, I didn't say anything."

"You better not have either." She thought I was stupid. Like I don't know what's happening. I was not about to let her leave me.

Aimee

He thought I didn't know he lied to his mother about why she couldn't visit. It made it hard for me because she and I had a good relationship. She contacted me to see what was going on and I had to cover. That broken arm was literally the lie of all lies to everyone. Friends and family alike. The problem with lying is keeping track of all the lies you told. I know we told her I broke my arm. I couldn't remember if we never said how it happened.

The only good thing that came from that night was the card Nurse Carol gave me. It was her information as well as information for a domestic violence support group. While I never went to the domestic violence group, I did text Nurse Carol and met up with her a few times. She became a good friend. I could actually be honest because she knew what was going on. I was so grateful that God sent her into my life.

"Hi Carol, it's Aimee."

"How are you?"

"It's hit the fan. He started back up again and this time I knew I needed to get my baby out. We went to my cousin's house."

"Are you okay?"

"I am. The baby is with my sister for the rest of the weekend. I am staying at a hotel to relax and just think."

"Let me know if you need anything. My door is always open to you and Addy."

"Thank you." It was good to have someone outside of my family that understood what I was going through.

I checked into a hotel. Darius paid for it, I asked for his help because I want Brian tracking me with my debit card purchase. I knew I needed to open up my own bank account. I didn't know where things were going, but I knew I had to start somewhere. Darius stayed with me for a while and we talked.

"Thanks for helping me."

"No thanks needed. Why? I just don't understand why." Darius said.

"This is why I never said anything. I can't answer these questions. I just don't know. I thought I was stronger than this. You know, you talk about these things with your girls. You say things like, I would never let a man hit me. That first time, I am leaving. The real deal is, you don't know how you will react until you are in it."

"I understand, but we all love you and would never want to see you experiencing this."

"D, I know. Believe me, I was afraid of telling you because I know you'd be ready to go for blood and I do not want you doing something that would ruin your life because of something happening in my life."

"I want to be honest." His tone changed and was softer. I had no idea what he was about to say.

"Okay."

"There was a time where I thought we would be together."

"Really?" I never thought he felt like this. He never said a word. He never even hinted toward feeling anything.

"Yeah. Don't sound so shocked."

"I would have never gotten that impression. You never said anything or behaved in a way that would make me think anything other than we were just friends."

"It was your freshman year in college and I came down to visit you. Remember?"

"Yeah, you came to hang for homecoming. We had a blast."

"We did and we slept in the bed together. That was when I knew, but got cold feet when I was going to say something. The next time, I decided to man up and say something was your graduation, but you introduced the family to Brian. I would never disrespect your relationship, so I left it alone."

"I don't know what to say."

"Don't say anything, except you are leaving Brian. I don't care who you are with, even if it isn't me. I don't want you hurt. It hurts that I didn't notice that something was wrong."

"I got really good at hiding things and lying."

"Aimee, please don't go back to this. Your life is worth more and I love you."

"I love you too, D.

I said good night to Darius after we sat talking for hours, laughing and eating pizza. I opened my journal to process this new intersection. My new reality of what was now my life meant taking action to leave the abusive relationship that had become my life.

Tonight, was fun. I spent time with my good friend, just talking and laughing. I haven't laughed so much in a long while. I haven't been so relaxed in a long time. Reminiscing about the old days and talking about what we hope our future would be. I realized; I still have dreams. They did not die. If anything, they have intensified. I have Addison to raise. While I am feeling all these feelings, I know I have a long road ahead of me. How do I move on? I love my husband. I wonder why sometimes he doesn't feel the same about me. That feeling of emptiness after he pummels me. The part I hate the most is when he climbs into bed and tries to cuddle with me or make love to me. Like where was that tenderness previously? Did you think about that before you put your hands on me? I am in a hotel room taking a break from my husband. I should not have to run from him or my home. This was not the life I thought I would be living. I know I need to get out, but how?

Lost
I've lost my faith.
It got lost between here and there.
Lost hope.
Heart empty because I just don't see it to believe it.
No faith in God.
Not in humanity.
I'm empty.
Lost on how this came to be.
Feeling deceived.
Handed a pipe dream... on prayers that have gone unanswered.
I do believe I've seen the worst of the worst.
Received my own testimony because the elders' stories weren't enough.
What did I gain?
Loss of love.
Alone and lonely.
Emptiness.
I am still lost!

When I woke the next morning, I decided that I would go to the support group Carol had told me about called *Healing Hands*. It was time for me to do something different. I decided to skip church for today and just rest. I called my sister to check in on Addy.

"My sister, I need you to pick up Addison from daycare tomorrow. I will come get her from you."

"Not a problem. You hear her making all that noise. How are you?"

"She's growing fast. I will pick her up from you after service. I think I am okay. I mean, I feel a little better. The swelling has gone down around my eye. My lip is still a bit fat. I have cover up and shades." The line got quiet, although I could still hear Addison making noises in the background.

"Andrea, you still there?"

"Yes, yes. I am."

"Are you crying?"

"I just don't understand why you didn't come to me. Or mom and dad." I could feel her hurt.

"My sister, it was hard to fathom that this was even happening, let alone tell the people who love me the most."

"I can understand that. I guess it's because we're so close that I thought you would have told me something like this was happening to you."

"I am your older sister. How can I tell my baby sister this? I am supposed to be protecting you and I couldn't even protect myself. But telling anyone was too embarrassing. I mean, here I am young, successful and now a mother, but I am constantly being abused by my *loving and caring* husband. This wasn't supposed to happen to me."

"I am just still baffled that my tough, strong sister didn't reach out for help."

"Exactly. I didn't believe I was one of those you know, weak people. I thought I was stronger than that. I thought..." My voice trailed off and I remained quiet.

"Anyone can be a survivor of intimate partner violence. Are you okay, sister?"

"No, no. I am not okay." I tried to keep myself together for so long, but I am glad I can be honest and let it out.

"I am proud of you."

"Why?" I didn't feel like I had done anything.

"You left. You protected Addison and you left."

"I really had no choice at this point. At the rate things were going, he was going to kill me. Besides, my baby doesn't deserve to grow up in toxic environment." I was finally regaining some power and control over myself. "Give her lots of kisses from me and cuddles. I love you."

"I love you too. I am here to listen. I got your back. Always." Having the support of my family right now was key. Especially since it was so hard to tell them anything to begin with.

Brian

I didn't know who she thought she was, but she was still my wife. I'd been calling and calling and no answer. Straight to voicemail, again. Just when I was about to try her number again, I heard the key in the door.

"Where have you been?" I yelled.

"I just needed time to think." She responded so calmly.

"Where is my daughter?"

"With my sister."

"Oh, so you were having sex then."

"What? How do you equate the two? You're crazy."

"You heard me. You stayed out all night and if my daughter is with your sister, you must have been getting fucked."

"Our daughter, Addison, is with my sister to give me a break. You can think what you want about the rest of it." Her tone pissed me off. I was fuming. Who did she think she was talking to? How dare she address me, her husband in that manner?! I deserved respect. I needed to remind her who I was and how she should address me. I grabbed her by the back of her head getting a tight grip on her hair. She quickly turned around slapping my hand away with force and it made me recoil, "If you think that is what we are going to do today, you got another thing coming."

"Oh shit, so you think you got things all under control now?" I was shocked, but she wasn't going to know that.

"No, I am just not tolerating this anymore."

"Tolerate. Bitch, don't get fucked up."

"Stop calling me names and if you touch me. I will dial 911."

We stared each other down for what seemed like hours. Believing she would call the police, I backed off. She did not appear to be bluffing and I had no desire to go to jail.

A week passed and it became apparent to me that I had lost her. I could see she had enough, but I couldn't help myself. I continued to antagonize her. I was not proud of the person I became; however I didn't know how or what to do next. It seemed like she spent more and more time out of the house. She always came home, but it was different. Aimee was never mean or rude, but she became stern. She didn't deny me time with Addison, but she also did not sleep in our room anymore and kept her distance. Conversation was kept at a minimal.

"How long are you going to keep this up?"

"Keep what up?"

"Are you plotting to leave?"

"I am not plotting anything."

"You can't leave me."

"Can't? I believe it is a matter of will or won't." I felt my blood boiling behind that comment. She thinks she can just walk out on our marriage? She had another thing coming.

"You better stop listening to all your friends and family putting that nonsense in your head about leaving me." She went to walk away I grabbed her arm.

"Brian, let me go. You need help." She snatched her arm away from me.

"Don't fucking tell me what to do. I don't need help." My hand slapped her face and I grabbed her arm, again, this time tighter. She was screaming for me to get off of her. I kept wailing on her and then the doorbell rang. "Go upstairs. NOW!"
I went to the door to find Mike there.

"What's up Mike?"

"You tell me. I heard you and Aimee yelling."

"Just an argument. Nothing major."

"You going to let me in? I came to see my god baby."

"I shouldn't because your ass didn't call. Addison is with her aunt."

"Yeah, whatever."

"Aimee was going to get her."

"I'll be back."

I went upstairs to find Aimee trying to calm down.

"Who is that?" Aimee asked.

"Mike. He came to see Addy. I told him she was with your sister, but you should show your face so he won't think anything."

"Think what? That you are whipping my ass regularly? That you are an abusive prick? Afraid your friends will know the real you. She was getting really bold and her mouth reckless. She needed to be reminded of who I was.

"Just get the fuck up and clean up and come down."

I went back down stairs and was shooting the shit with Mike. It seemed a little too long for her to be up there. About 20 minutes later, she came downstairs with bags.

"Hey Mike."

"Sis, what happened?" She had not cleaned up. She just packed up.

"Your boy happened. Can you drop me off?"

Mike never looked at me. "Yeah, anywhere you want to go."

"Bro." It was all he said to me. Mike left his beer and they walked out the house.

I was alone, again. That night, I got on my knees and prayed. I never do that, but who else would I talk to? God would listen, right? Maybe He wouldn't. I had become something I hated. I saw my mom get beat up by her ex-boyfriend, so many times and for years. She would say, "*Baby, don't worry. Mama's okay.*" She was not okay to me. Broken ribs one time, another time her tailbone. She still went to work, cooked and cleaned. The neighbors knew. Family knew, no one ever stepped in. One day, she woke me up in the middle of the night with our bags packed and we left. Never saw that man again until I had become him.

Aimee

Mike didn't ask many questions. We rode in lots of silence. He asked, "Sis, how long?" When the car stopped at a red light, Mike was full of conversation. Guys process differently, this experience had truly taught me that.

"It started pretty much after we got married. It stopped during pregnancy and then it started back up again."

"I am so sorry, sis. I had no idea. It does explain some of his behaviors. I just could never think anything like this." Mike couldn't have had an idea, just like many others. To see us together, no one would know. Behind closed doors, our relationship was something totally different.

"Is he the reason you broke your arm?"

"Yeah."

"Damn. I can't believe my boy, my brother, my frat was doing this to you. I'm almost embarrassed that none of us were paying enough attention. Does his mother know?"

"I don't think so. I am always covering up and lying. There are so many lies Mike. Like the lies almost feel second nature. I know people thought some things but no one outright asked. My coworker, Rodriguez did because he saw me daily, but I was afraid to be honest. All of you, while not my brothers, treat me like a sister."

"That is how it is supposed to be. We can't tolerate violence in our community. Especially if it is someone you love and have a personal relationship with. That will always be my brother, but Brian is no exception to any of that. The only reason I didn't stomp a mudhole in his back is because of the relationship. Plus violence is not the answer to violence."

When I got to my parent's house, my sister was there with Addison. Mike helped me with my things. Then there were more questions. I was afraid, but I didn't want to go out the City to Liza's. When my parents saw me, they were mortified.

"Look at you." My mother yelled as she wrapped her arms around me. She began to cry as did I.

"Ma, I am okay." I actually meant it this time although, I probably didn't look it.

"Girl, not from where I'm standing." She hugged my neck tightly before letting me go. She disappeared to get supplies to clean my face.

"Aimee how long has this been happening?" My dad, the patriarch of our family would want to know every detail about the last three years. Why is this everyone's first question? What difference does that make? "I think I need to go have a talk with Brian."

"Dad, that won't be necessary. Mike came by to see Addy and I think that was enough. I knew Mike's visit would not be short, so I'd made good use of the time I had and packed Addy's and my bags. Living with him had become too much to endure, especially with Addy. I knew it would be safe to leave while Mike was there and I wanted his friend, our friend to see him for who he was. I was done protecting him." I have never seen my father look at me like that. If I could have melted into the floor I would have. I think he was more hurt that I didn't say anything to him and my mother. Even after talking, I could see my father still wanted to go to my house, but I asked him not to. It was a hard conversation, but one that I knew I couldn't avoid forever.

Tomorrow I was going back to the group for the second time. For tonight, I just needed a good night's sleep. Before I rested my eyes, I opened that journal.

Attempting to understand his motive. Why he hates me so much? What did he ever see in me, if he was just going to mentally and physically harm me? I may never get the answers to any of my questions. I don't know if I need the answers. My heart aches and I wonder how he would react if it was a man putting their hands on Addy. I clearly am of no importance to him. He obviously does not respect me. I will continue to have a relationship with my mother-in-law. I love her. She has been nothing but kind and loving toward me and she adores Addy. I will probably call her soon. I can't imagine what that conversation will be like.

The next day seemed to drag. Anxiety, nervousness, fear were the major emotions I was feeling. When I got to *Healing Hands*, I was surprised at how many people were there at this group. That was when I really knew I wasn't alone. Then Carol walked in the room.

"You finally came." She said to me.

"I did a few weeks ago too, but…"

"Yes, I told you that you were not alone." We hugged for what seemed like such a long time. It was only like three people the day I came and I got cold feet and left out before it even started. We got seats and chatted while others arrived, most of them saying hello to Carol as they drifted in.

The facilitator, Ms. Dion, introduced herself and then everyone in the circle did as well. Ms. Dion spoke of the power wheel and I could recognize myself in the cycle. There was a moment where the tears just ran down my face. We talked about safety; this was where I was paying lots of attention. Then the part I was completely dreading, sharing. Ms. Dion made it clear that if we did not want to share, we did not have to. I felt like I dodged a bullet.

"Is there anyone who would like to share?" Ms. Dion said. The survivors in the room shifted in their seats. Everyone waiting for the brave soul to go first. Then the space began to fill with voices:

The first lady that spoke was Eva Lynn. "I felt isolated. No one would talk to me because everyone was afraid of my boyfriend. He would always say no other man would want me. Started calling me ugly. At first, it was all verbal abuse. The physical abuse came later, and I fought back. I didn't think anything was wrong. My family would say, *what did you do*? I never understood that. How they stood by and never helped me. The thing that made me wake up was watching my son and daughter play fighting as if it were us. *Healing Hands* helped me to prepare for getting out. Safely."

"Thank you for sharing, Eva Lynn. Creating a safety plan is important, especially when children are involved. Sometimes getting out can be detrimental to survivors." Ms. Dion scanned the room for the next person to share. "Is there anyone else who would like to share this evening?" On the heels of her question, a voice began speaking.

Her name was Stacy: "I watched my mom be abused by my dad for years, right up until the day she died by his hands. Then I got into a similar relationship, mostly because I thought it was the way it was supposed to be. One day, in a heated argument he took a bottle from the side of the bed. It had urine in it. He threw it on me. I felt so disgusted and that day, I lost it. I picked up the first thing I could grab and started swinging. It was a screwdriver. I sure did stab him with it. When I left, I was followed by him for six months. He would show up at CVS, the doctor's office, my school, and I knew he was aware of where I moved to. My cousin said that she saw him in the store one day, when she was coming over. Eventually it stopped. I guess he found someone else. It has been hard being in my new relationship because I am always on guard and waiting for the other shoe to drop sort of speak."

"The impact of trauma can manifest immediately or years later. The impact can often be long lasting throughout the life span. The key is addressing it, which is no easy feat. It can play out in the smallest of interactions. The goal is to become aware and manage it as opposed to it managing you.

Anyone else?" It was quiet. I hung my head staring at my fingernails. Unsure if I was ready to share or comfortable to say a thing. We were trusting this space to share some of the most difficult times in our lives with people who were basically strangers. One of the two men in the room raised his hand. "Yes Tim."

"I don't know when it started. It just happened one day. My boyfriend and I just started going at it. We almost took turns. It was abusive. Toxic. Seemed like everyone knew. All of our friends, his family, my family. In the end, I knew this was not what I wanted for my life and I made sure to make a clean break. People think it doesn't happen in same sex relationships, especially between men but, it does." The interventions are different if you call the cops. The response is often inappropriate. One cop said, *aren't you a man, fight back.* Then the other called me a pussy. You can't trust law enforcement to be a source of support.

"Tim, thanks for showing up and sharing. As you said, it could be difficult for the LGBTQ community to engage with law enforcement and ask for help especially with the intersectionality of being a person of color. People of color don't always trust law enforcement to begin with." Ms. Dion said. Is there anyone else?

Carol shifted in her seat and then started talking. "At 14 years old, my father punched me in the face. I don't know what I said to warrant that.

By anyone's standards, I was a typical teenager. I did not tell anyone. It lasted for three years. I had no place to go and because he was my source of income, I couldn't just leave. Right after my 17th birthday, a big fight broke out. He was accusing me of sleeping around. I was still a virgin. Where he got that idea from was beyond me. It was hard. I had no choice, but to go to school with my face cut, a black eye and arms bruised. I couldn't hide any longer. I was ashamed, not understanding how the man who The day after that fight, I walked into school and literally right into my principal. She looked at me and said, come to my office. She called in the school social worker, the guidance counselor and Mrs. Bradford, my English teacher. My school's social worker was awesome in helping me press charges. In the end, I survived it and realized that this was not how love was shown. I am glad to have a husband who loves me tenderly. He is the opposite of everything my father was. I forgave my father, which took a long time."

Ms. Dion, ready to end the session, "Thanks Carol. Childhood abuse often goes unreported, especially with teens because they have learned how to hide. The key is having a strong support system." She looked around the room and smiled at each person, including me. Crossing her legs, she said, "I want to thank you all for sharing and coming out this evening."

I had no intent on saying anything. My mouth started moving. "Ms. Dion, is it okay if I say something?"

"Sure."

"I want to read something I wrote last night." I stood up, butterflies in my stomach and began.

Speak
Today, I am struggling to find my voice.
It won't let me speak my truth. Mouth open and primed to spew thoughtful words, but the hope of the volume being raised,
BLEAK. So, it shall be.
Hiding behind hurt and hopelessness.
Hanging onto pride that won't let you see that my heart bleeds.
Life having loss of meaning.
Love dying.
Strangled, becoming lifeless.
I struggle to find my voice to speak words of wisdom.
I am quietly contemplating how to crawl out this shell to say what is on my mind, in my heart, down in my spirit.
Trying to find my way back to me. The one that matters.
Taking a front and center seat in my life.
My voice slowly peaks, groans from belly aching silence, finding low level tones, pitch up to mid volume... Finally reaching full blast to tell my story. Speaking things into existence, saying things as though they are. Pages no longer empty, filled with Dreams. Spoken.

Book Club Discussion Questions

Part One

1. Do you feel Justin was too harsh after the encounter with Kasey's mother? Why or why not?
2. Do you think Kasey's pregnancy impacted the chances of reconciliation? What would you do?
3. Kasey's relationship with her mother bore a weight that almost ruined her relationship with Justin. Does one's relationship with his or her parents impact his or her romantic relationships? How?

Part Two

1. Do you think Hunter was right in not sharing his past history regarding his high school girlfriend's abortion with Camille?

2. Do you feel that Hunter's resistance to therapy is typical of black men in general? Why or why not?
3. What thoughts do you think were going through Hunter and Camille's mind when they were at their regular check up only to find out that there was no heartbeat? What do you imagine Camille was thinking knowing she had to deliver her baby still born?

Part Three

1. Kristen and Sarah seem to harbor family secrets, but only Kristen's secrets surfaced in her relationship. What are your thoughts on Sarah's relationship with her family? Is it something Kristen should have known about? Why or why not?
2. Kristen's ex, Karen, seemed obsessive and even dangerous as time progressed before the assault, but Kristen was too ashamed to speak up. At what point in a past relationship is enough *enough*?
3. Kristen broke up with Sarah at the hospital after her assault, and Sarah seemed more upset over the break-up than the assault. Do you think Kristen made a wise decision? What are your thoughts on Sarah's reaction?

Part Four

1. How hard do you think it was for Aimee to keep up all the lies to her family and friends?
2. What do you think Brian's mother would have said if she found out that he was being abusive to Aimee? Do you think she would have blamed herself for it? Why or why not?
3. Do you think Nurse Carol overstepped her boundaries by giving Aimee her contact information?

About the Author

Verkeya Lanece is a native New Yorker and a licensed Master Social Worker. She is the founder of Verkeya Speaks, which a community organization created for panel discussion on various topics, including, but not limited to infertility and child loss. As a professional speaker, she has delivered messages on grief, loss and bereavement at New York University and Columbia University.

Verkeya Lanece is the mother of a baby angel, Kaleb and actively parenting her five-year-old, Kaiden.

You can follow her on Facebook Verkeya Speaks and Instagram **@verkeya_speaks** or visit her website www.verkeyaspeaks.com.